GOODBYE,
Granny Dix

GOODBYE,
Granny Dix

A Novel by Lynda Allison
FOREWORD BY NONA FREEMAN

Goodbye, Granny Dix

by Lynda Allison

©1991 Word Aflame Press
Hazelwood, MO 63042

Cover Design by Tim Agnew

Printed by

Library of Congress Cataloging-in-Publication Data

Allison, Lynda.
      Goodbye, Granny Dix : a novel / by Lynda Allison.
          p.   cm.
      ISBN 0-932581-82-X
      I. Title.
      PS3551.L456G66 1991
      813'.54—dc20   90-29320
                                             CIP

Contents

Lynda Allison adroitly uses moving, well-written stories based on facts to crusade against ominous tides of evil that assault our world. I sincerely appreciate and wholeheartedly endorse her clarion voice against abortion—the wholesale murder scheme regarded as "legal and respectable" by many.

In *Goodbye, Granny Dix,* Lynda courageously deals with another villainous plan, *euthanasia*—so-called mercy killing of the elderly—not yet legal but rapidly moving toward general acceptance. Observe the irony of a murder scheme propagated behind the tender word *mercy,* an essential requisite of our salvation!

Since Christians need to be aware of this diabolic plot now forming against the aged, I strongly recommend that you read *Goodbye, Granny Dix*—and PRAY.

Nona Freeman

Preface

Goodbye, Granny Dix is not a comedy. It's not even a funny story. It is a sad but very real commentary on our world. But it is also a story of triumph, because in it we see that each time, every time, Jesus Christ is the Victor!

You will see as you read through these pages that this book is not about cases of terminal illness in which people discontinue heroic efforts that merely postpone the inevitable, such as artificial life-support systems for a dying or brain-dead person. Sometimes this is referred to as "pulling the plug." Instead, this book talks about two very different things: one is to place a dying loved one in the hands of God and let Him make the life-or-death decision; the other, euthanasia, is to set oneself up as God, usurping His authority by forcing decisions that are absolutely none of our business.

No discussion of euthanasia ("mercy killing") would be complete without exploring the issue of abortion. They go together. Abortion creates a mentality, or mindset, that paves the way for euthanasia.

I have never been an eighty-year-old in Granny Dix's shoes, of course, but I have been asked if this novel really presents Lynda Allison in disguise. Well, yes and no. I did not "have" to get married, nor did a daughter of mine conceive out of wedlock. But I was an older student, a licensed pilot, and a magazine editor, and I was married to a millionaire who drove me to distraction. And the accounts of attempted suicide and abortion are written straight from my heart.

Those two chapters were particularly painful for me to write because it meant reliving a part of my past I had once laid to rest. But without them, this prolife story would not be complete. I knew I had to take the risk because far too many women, even some sitting on our own church pews, are caught in this death trap; how can I sit silently by and watch them hurt? I must speak out, and nothing speaks like a life. In this case, my own life. And my own healing, in the hands of a loving God.

These experiences, although so devastating at the time, can be used for good today. I would go through the pain all over again, if I knew that someday God would be able to use it for the benefit of others. I see that all things do indeed work together for good to those who love God, and He has called me to this purpose. But I had to reach the place where I would allow God into the secret rooms of my heart so that He could heal and make me whole. In finding my life's work, I have found completeness. You, too, can find this place in Jesus.

I have met with some criticism because of the realities I write about in my books, but for the most part, I have been warmly received. Either way, I will continue to speak out at every opportunity, because He is the One who receives the glory, and little lives are being saved. I also would like to thank Word Aflame Press for so graciously providing me this avenue of expression.

1

Grand Entrance

Amy Harper glanced at her watch, a wave of relief flooding over her. It looked as though the worst of the weather was behind her now, and in just a few more minutes she should be touching down at the Lawton airport. If only her fuel held out! Her nerves were already ragged from fighting the weather for the last two hours. The stormy headwinds had guzzled her gas and upset her calculations, and she wasn't sure just how much fuel she had left. As a new pilot with only 150 hours of logged time, this had undoubtedly been the longest, hardest trip in her flying experience, and all she could think about now was a hot bath and a mug of strong, black coffee.

But she couldn't escape the sinking feeling that she should have listened to that lineboy back in Sacramento. "Top it off, Ms. Harper?"

"Don't bother, thanks," Amy had said. "I've got enough gas to make it back into Lawton okay."

"Can't be too careful, though."

"I know, but I'm in a hurry." Famous last words, Amy thought. How many other pilots lived—or didn't live —to regret saying those very words?

She felt she had to get away from the oppressiveness of her mother's awful situation, but also to get home! Four days in the big city away from her family was enough. And who could have predicted these headwinds?

Now that things had settled down for a respite, she felt herself relaxing in spite of her uneasiness about the critical fuel situation. It was calm now, and the instruments were back to normal. Amy's dark, brooding eyes looked out over the vast expanse of land. It was a late March day, and the slight haze cast a wonderland glow over the land below. There were patches of green and brown, and skinny, crooked lines of gray that were actually rivers and streams. Now they were rapidly becoming enshrouded in the deep, dense darkness of twilight. The early nightfall lowered the visibility, which was already in the danger zone.

Amy loved flying. She enjoyed the solitude, the peace, that could only be found at eight thousand feet, up and away from shrilling telephones and teenaged daughters and crochety old professors demanding more and more when she had already given all she had to give. Peace? Amy smiled, remembering the violence she had just flown through. At one point, the updrafts had been so fierce that she had had to lower the landing gear to get enough drag to descend below the clouds that had suddenly enveloped her with no warning, no warning at all. She knew she'd better land soon, or she would be back in more weather. The storm was hurrying along behind her.

Amy was exhausted. And homesick. She missed her family! Thirteen-year-old Bethany. Fresh and bright faced, she was the light of Amy's life. And Jennifer, just turned eighteen and approaching high school graduation. Mature for her years, she had been such a help when Amy decided to go back to school four years ago. She had pitched right in, helping with the housework and raising little Bethany. Now that Amy and Cliff could afford a live-in housekeeper, Miriam had taken these responsibilities off the young girl.

And Cliff. He had been forced to quit school in the eighth grade and go to work to support his mother. But instead of the experiences hindering him, he had developed grit and determination to make something of himself. He had finished business college, then law school, and now he had just acquired his first million dollars in the field of real estate development. So gentle and tender, Cliff was. Amy frowned. But was he really? She would find out soon enough when she dropped the bombshell about her mother. Poor Granny Dix.

A sudden gust of wind buffeted the little Cessna, shattering Amy's reverie. Ordinarily this was such a gorgeous time of day, with lights scattering throughout the darkening expanse, twinkling here and there, winking at her in a warm welcome home. But tonight . . .well, she had hoped to land long before nightfall. She was nearly two hours overdue, and the storm seemed to be getting closer. She'd hate to be caught in that; it looked awful.

The radio had been erratic ever since she had left Sacramento. Unsuccessful in raising the approach control, she now reached over to try again for the local tower.

That was when she heard it. The engine sputtered. Just a little gasp. But just enough to cause Amy to suck in her breath in apprehension.

There it was again. Cough. Beads of perspiration began to break out on her forehead, and she found herself searching the ground below for signs of the airport. With any luck, she should be able to make it in even with an empty fuel tank. That was the most she could hope for at this point. A single-engine aircraft flying VFR in instrument conditions after legal sunset—well, Amy wished now she had logged more hours in the air!

She pressed the microphone to her mouth, "Lawton Tower, this is 97 Zulu, can you read me? Over." As her eyes scanned the earth, she realized something was very wrong. Where were the usual landmarks? She straightened up, tense, taut. Could she have drifted off course? What on earth had happened to the airport?

"Rats!" The silence that replaced the drone of the engines was eerie, and Amy knew there was only one thing to do: land in some cow pasture somewhere. She began trimming the plane, adjusting dials and knobs, as the silence grew absolutely deafening. "Lawton Tower, can you read me? I'm out of fuel. Over, please."

Amy's eyes scanned the earth as it suddenly started racing towards her safe cocoon within the cockpit. She recognized absolutely nothing below, just saw a haphazard array of lights. There was no time to circle around looking; she would have to make some kind of landing fast. Her fingers trembled as she went through the futile motions of trimming the plane and trying to set it in some sort of orderly fashion. Her legs were fiercely vibrating as she manipulated the rudder pedals.

Suddenly a sound came shattering into the cabin, a rattling sound of violent static. "97 Zulu, this is Lawton Tower. Go ahead."

But it was too late now for the radio. Amy had both hands full, and the trees were coming directly toward her. *Oh, God, no, not trees!* she thought, her mind tumbling with memories of a friend being impaled by a tree last year. Impaled, dead, never to see his family again. . . . Cut all switches, this is it.

"97 Zulu? Can you read me? This is Lawton Tower." Closer and closer the ground was racing up to meet her. The plane was spinning, and yet there was nothing she could do at this point. "97 Zulu, over please."

With one last, hopeless glance in the direction of the radio, Amy yelled out, knowing she could not be heard. "I'm going down!" Then, with a deep breath, she plummeted to the ground, lost in the awful sounds of crashing glass and metal. Mercifully, the world blacked out before the tiny plane came to its final resting place.

* * * * *

Less than three miles away at the airport, Cliff Harper paced the dingy little waiting room of Anderson Aviation. Periodically he would stand at the plate-glass window, his eyes scanning the dark sky for his wife. The radio kept barking out information about other flights and other pilots and other situations, but nothing came over about Amy. Cliff's fingers jiggled around in his pockets for some change, and he studied the menu on the coffee machine as though it were a legal document involving his vast estate. Finally he put in his quarter and retrieved a plastic cup of black liquid. He was already coffee-logged, but what else was there to do when your wife's flight was overdue and the last communication had never been answered?

Jim Anderson, the owner of the little fixed-base operation, came tumbling inside, the wind threatening to tear the door from its hinges. With a mighty yanking motion, Jim managed to shut the door and, rubbing his bare hands together rapidly, spat: "Ugh! It's gusty out there!" He crossed the tiny room to the heater, backing up to it as though it were a fireplace putting out clouds of warm and comforting heat. "Nothing from Amy yet?" he asked, glancing in Cliff's direction.

Cliff shook his head. He and Jim had been friends for a long time, having learned to fly together about ten years ago. In Cliff's business as a real estate developer, he had occasion to fly often, and he kept his planes in a hangar here at Jim's place.

"This is the craziest weather I've seen in a long time," Jim went on, trying to keep a light, conversational tone.

"I don't think Amy's got any experience in this kind of weather," said Cliff.

"Ah, she'll do fine, wait and see."

But Cliff continued to brood. "My animals won't like it. The horses, especially, get awfully skittish."

"I just flew over your spread, Cliff. It's still quiet out that way. Might just go around it."

"That sure would be nice, I—" Sudden crackling sounds from the radio filled the background, and a voice came out, loud and clear. "Anderson Aviation? This is

Ground Control."

Jim covered the room in two giant steps, darted behind the counter, and grabbed the mike. "Anderson here, what you got?"

"They just spotted what looks like a downed plane out near the quarries. Contact Suber Aviation. Over and out."

"Roger!" Jim said, swiveling to the telephone on the other side of the marred old wooden desk. When he replaced the phone, he turned to Cliff, who was leaning anxiously against the counter. "C'mon, let's go." And with that, they were out the door.

2

New Love

Jennifer and Billy . . . Billy and Jennifer . . .

Jennifer Harper, Amy's older daughter, gently traced the words in the dirt with slim, long fingers. She kept her eyes averted, as if embarrassed to look at Billy as he watched her write the magic words. She and Billy Eversole had been horseback riding over the Harper spread and were resting by the creek before calling it a day. It was time for supper, and the chilled evening was setting in fast.

At last she glanced up at him, peering from beneath long, black eyelashes. Her dark eyes shone with the early glow of first love, and excitement danced like flames of fire when the eyes of the two young people met.

Billy's large, tanned hand reached out to close over Jennifer's. Her heart skipped a beat, and the smile that had been playing around the corners of her full, pink lips froze. "I love you, Jen. I need you to marry me."

The waters of the creek rushed by, and Jennifer

watched them with feigned interest. The breeze that had been softly sweeping across the open field, gently teasing the leaves of the tree that formed an umbrella over the young pair, was growing stronger, rougher. Their horses had been standing by patiently but were beginning to grow restless with the smell of a storm that seemed determined to assault the area. "It's getting cold out here," she said with a slight shiver.

"You love me, too, Jennifer Harper," Billy went on. He removed his leather jacket and gingerly laid it across her shoulders. "I know you do."

"We'd better head back."

"In a minute. Will you marry me?"

"You're too old for me," came a playful drawl.

Billy grinned. "Ah, but you need someone older. Wiser, experienced."

"Even so, my parents would never agree to our getting married. At least not until you've settled down and gotten a job."

"I've got a job."

Jennifer smiled. "Cowboys don't get paid enough. Not even with the raise Daddy just gave you. My folks would have to know that you can support me and will let me start college in the fall."

Billy's shoulders slumped. "I like the work I'm doing, Jen. I was born to work outdoors. I'd probably go berserk stuck behind a desk somewhere."

Jennifer loved the lines of his face. They were lines made by wind and sun, lines on a face that had spent much time in the outdoor world, raising horses and herding cattle on the Harper ranch. A strong face, handsome in an obscure and rugged way. Jennifer loved the very sight of it. She loved that smile, the way it made his eyes brighten and crinkle at the corners.

"But you're right," he went on. "Your parents would never let you marry a hired hand."

"My parents are not snobs," she protested.

Billy was lost for a moment in reflection. "Well," he ventured, "would they feel better about it if I worked in the statehouse? Maybe Rich can find something for me to do when he goes in, come January."

"There's no guarantee, you know," said Jennifer, "that Rich will even win the election. Anyway, we won't even know that until November!"

"I know."

Billy and Jennifer both were committed to Rich Meyers and the brand of leadership he would bring to the state. Solid, competent, honest leadership. Billy seemed to hold some sort of abiding conviction that his candidate would indeed become the next governor.

"Well, we'll see," she said. "But my parents do like you, Billy. They've said many times how much they admire your work. They respect you, too."

"But not as a son-in-law."

Jennifer shrugged. "Well, I adore you," she said, "and I'd marry you in a minute!"

He grinned and rolled his eyes around playfully. "Then let's do it."

Jennifer's breath caught at the realization of what he was saying. Without another word, she pushed herself up from the ground and started moving toward Lady Dawn, her own prize Appaloosa mare. "We'd better get back," she called over her shoulder. "Those winds are getting bad." Billy soundlessly followed her, and they mounted their horses and started trotting across the field in the direction of the house.

Jennifer loved horses and the feel of the mammoth, quivering flesh beneath her. There was an exhilarating sense of accomplishment in conquering the animal, a thrilling sense of the power of man—or woman—over beast. A chill was settling in as the sun disappeared over the western knoll, and with a quick glance at each other, the young people began galloping back to the house.

* * * * *

Miriam, the housekeeper, was calling across the field as the pair finished bedding their horses down and made their way from the barn. "Jennifer," Miriam was calling, "your grandmother is holding on the phone for you."

"Granny Dix!" Jennifer broke into an excited run, trailed by Billy. Seeing that he was temporarily forgotten, Billy turned and headed down the hill in the opposite direction toward his own cabin. He would retrieve his jacket at supper.

Inside the house, Jennifer grasped the phone. "Hi, Granny Dix!"

"Hello there, child," came the soft, Southern voice over the line. After all these years of being away from her native Carolina, Granny Dix still had that graceful accent. "Miriam tells me your mother's not back yet. You haven't heard anything from her?"

"No ma'am. Daddy went to the airport to pick her

up, so I imagine they went out to dinner or something. But how are you, Granny Dix?"

"Much better, dear. I'll be ready to leave the hospital in a week or so."

"Great! We've all been so worried about you."

"Never a reason to worry," she said. "The good Lord's got everything under control." Jennifer did not understand much about the Lord, but she could tell, even over the phone, that Granny Dix had that joyful gleam in her eye, the same one she got every time she talked about the Lord. "My house is all gone, though, Jenny, and everything in it. Burned down. Even Sugar."

"I'm sorry." Granny Dix had been phoning often lately, and even though Jennifer had heard the story many times, she always listened attentively as her grandmother recounted the tragedy.

She had apparently left some oatmeal simmering on the stove and dozed off in the living room while enjoying one of her many cassette tapes. When she awoke, she barely had time to get out the front door, and she ended up with a mixture of first- and second-degree burns over her lower arms and hands. The worst damage, though, had been to her lungs, from smoke inhalation. Jennifer heard that the older woman would probably not have been injured at all had she not taken time to gather some of her possessions into what she called her ditty-bag. She had also wasted valuable time searching for her beloved Persian cat, Sugar. Sugar ended up perishing in the fire after all, huddled in the corner of what had once been the hall linen closet.

Amy had spent a lot of time flying back and forth the

past few weeks while Granny Dix was in the hospital. She seemed to be recovering, but Jennifer wondered if she would ever recover from losing all her cherished possessions. Especially Sugar. She had loved her loyal, old pet for fifteen years. With over fifty years of living in the same house, she had accumulated a lot of clutter, keepsakes, and mementoes. Amy herself had been born in that house.

"Mom said something about you not having any insurance."

Dismayed silence on the other end of the line. "Oh dear, would you believe it lapsed just six months ago? I forgot to pay the premium. It just completely slipped my mind."

"Oh, Granny Dix . . ."

"Your grandfather always took care of those things, dear. I guess it's hard to teach an old dog new tricks."

Jennifer felt helpless frustration. She loved her grandmother, and it hurt to see how forgetful the older woman had become. Leaving food cooking on the stove, forgetting her insurance premiums. And now what? She would soon be eighty years old and wouldn't be getting any better. Jennifer sighed.

"Well, dear," Granny Dix went on, "I was just checking to see if your mother got back safely. I heard reports on the radio about some nasty weather between here and there and—well, don't bother her with this old lady's worrying. I guess I'm just old-fashioned enough not to trust airplanes—especially those tiny little things your mama flies."

Jennifer smiled to herself as she hung up the phone.

Granny Dix always did that to her, always made her laugh and feel better. There was just something about her that cheered everybody up. Even when Granny Dix was tired and worn out herself, she had a twinkle in her eye that uplifted those around her.

With a spring in her step, Jennifer padded down the thickly carpeted hallway to her room. On the way, she passed Bethany's room. The door was open, and the younger sister was sprawled on her bed doing homework. "Hey, Squirt."

Bethany looked up. Ignoring the use of the nickname, she asked, "What's going to happen to Granny Dix?"

Jennifer shrugged. "I'm not sure. She says she's almost ready to get out of the hospital."

"She's not going to come here, is she? I mean, live with us?"

"Of course she is. She doesn't have anywhere else to go."

Bethany bit her lip as though wanting to say something else. Jennifer studied her younger sister carefully. "What's the matter?"

"Nothing. Except I don't think Daddy'll like her coming here."

"He'll get used to it."

"Besides, there's not enough room—unless she sleeps with you."

"Bethany," Jennifer mused sadly, "you're so spoiled and selfish."

"No, I'm not."

Jennifer looked at her little sister for a long moment. "You're also getting a little fat, aren't you?"

Bethany tossed her head, throwing long, blond curls down her back. "That's mean."

"Sorry."

"You were gone a long time with Billy," Bethany went on. Her deep-blue eyes flashed with unspoken accusation.

"At least we made it back before dark."

"Yeah? By whose definition?" Bethany snapped. "You know Mom doesn't like it, you being alone so much with him. Besides, she wants you to date Jeffrey King."

"Oh, Jeffrey King," sniffed Jennifer. "You're just a mama's girl. Which reminds me . . . what were you doing out walking in the pastures with Gary Summers?" Bethany did not answer. Wordlessly, she started doodling on her math book cover. Jennifer folded her arms and looked at her sister through slitted eyes. "Bethany. You're too young to be taking walks like that with guys."

At this, Bethany's head jerked up. Her eyes flashed at her sister in a way that Jennifer had never seen before. "Who says I'm too young?"

"Well, *I* say it."

"Our Family Life teacher says it's good to build relationships and be close to each other."

"I hope you don't listen to all that garbage they dish out," said Jennifer.

"They're teachers, and they should know what they're talking about," pouted Bethany. "And besides, Mom and Dad don't care."

"You child! Bethany, just because they don't make you live by strict prison rules does not mean they don't care! They do care. And you better be careful." Bethany continued doodling on her book, and a long moment of silence finally passed. "Say," drawled Jennifer, "can you keep a secret?"

Bethany's eyes sparked with interest, her plump young body springing up on the bed. Throwing aside notebook and pencils, she leaned forward. "What is it?"

Jennifer looked up and down the hallway briefly and then stepped just inside the door of her sister's room. "Billy," she whispered, savoring the news she was getting ready to report, "Billy asked me to marry him."

Bethany's mouth opened. "Marry him?"

"Sh-h-h!" warned Jennifer. "Not so loud! Miriam might hear you."

"Oh, Miriam, she's just the maid."

"Housekeeper."

"Mom and Dad would throw fits."

Jennifer's face fell. "I know."

"Billy's nice," admitted Bethany. "What did you tell him?"

Jennifer's face took on that same glow it had earlier beside the creek. "I've got a plan," she said, rolling her eyes in secret delight, "but I can't tell you about it."

"Yes! Yes!"

Jennifer shook her head. "Because you talk too much, Squirt."

"I don't either."

"You talk too much," Jennifer repeated, "and *this* plan requires the absolute, utmost secrecy. Stick around; you'll find out."

With that, Jennifer spun around and disappeared down the hall to her room. Bethany stared after her, not even daring to wonder what her big sister had up her sleeve this time.

3

Home Sweet Home

Amy huddled there, shivering in the little cockpit, enveloped in total blackness. Unable to get the seat belt unlatched, she felt an awful, pinned-down helplessness.

She peered into the darkness, unable to see anything very clearly. She could make out the bashed-in windshield staring at her from a crooked, grotesque angle. Remembering those last few moments before the crash, Amy was shocked that she was still alive. The last thing she remembered was waiting for whatever it would feel like to be impaled by a tree. She did not know how long she had been here, because the clock had stopped on impact: 6:08. Amy realized she must have lost consciousness, but she had the feeling she couldn't have been out for very long. The only thing she knew for sure was that the wild ride was finally over.

The soft sound of rain drizzling onto the broken aircraft could barely be heard above the strong, howling wind. It looked, Amy thought, as if the rain might be

29

setting in for the night. She shivered again, and her fingers searched futilely for the little jacket that had been lying on the passenger seat. She was cold! And getting sore.

She fumbled again with the seat belt, and finally the latch clicked loose. A low groan escaped from her lips as she made a quick movement toward the door. Every muscle straining and aching, she pushed against the battered door until she saw it was not going to open. Her heart sank as she realized she was trapped inside this black coffin!

Exasperated, with waves of frustration flooding over her, Amy sighed and leaned back into the seat. The loneliness was awful! She couldn't remember the last time she had ever felt this kind of loneliness. Abandoned, empty, abused. All alone in the middle of the woods somewhere, she did not know if anyone would ever find her. The sound of the wind was eerie, and it was blowing against the little plane with a frightening fierceness. Amy thought it would be such shameful irony to have gotten down onto the ground safely, only to be blown away by the wind.

Without any warning, her cheeks became drenched with the tears that were spilling over. She had been wanting to cry and fighting it for several days now. All the hurt concerning her mother's situation had been eating away at her. It seemed so hopeless that all she had wanted to do was get back home and talk with Cliff and get all this madness worked out. But then, just thinking of having to tell Cliff made the agony even worse.

Now Amy just sat there in the blackness, eyes closed, allowing the luxury of the emotion. At last, she had given in to it. It was the only thing, she thought, that was keeping her sane right now. She remained there, unmoving, letting tears roll quietly until she dozed off.

She awoke with a start to the sound of voices. She sat up straight, stiff. Her first instinct was that of danger. She could almost smell it. The isolation, the dark night. The rain, and that awful, horrifying wind. She was at the mercy of whoever was out there, whatever kind of *thing* might be stalking around in these woods.

Suddenly the plane made a violent rocking motion as someone jumped up onto the wing. The voices again. Amy held her breath. She was afraid to breathe, afraid that whoever it was might hear her. There were voices again, but the wind drowned them out. Her head was spinning with the horror of helplessness.

Without any warning, a sliver of light began oozing around the cockpit. A flashlight! She held her breath as it made its merciless search, shutting her eyes tightly with the childlike hope that if she couldn't see it, maybe it couldn't see her.

Then, all of a sudden, she heard it. The sound of her name! Amy burst into joyous tears. Cliff!

He said something else as he and Jim Anderson began working the door loose, but she couldn't hear it. The sudden burst of air was a shock, almost taking her breath away, and the sound was deafening. With one giant motion, Cliff swooped her up, jumped off the wing, and sped down the woody, rocky path to Jim Anderson's waiting truck. Jim, after making a final check and securing what was left of the craft, followed, dropping his large frame into his front seat. "She needs Memorial."

Amy sat up tall and straight between the two men.

GOODBYE, GRANNY DIX

The thought of an emergency room with the nauseating odors and sickening sounds repulsed her. "No hospital; I'm fine."

"I understand," Cliff said. "You might *feel* okay, but we don't know what's underneath."

"Cliff, I just spent four days hanging around my mother's awful hospital, and I refuse to go to one here."

Jim Anderson started the engine and gave her a swift, sidewise glance. "I feel a certain responsibility here," he said, "and I would hate to see you go without medical help in case something's wrong. It wouldn't hurt to be checked over."

Amy was resolute. "I accept responsibility for myself. I'm a little sore—who wouldn't be? But I'm fine. Truly I am. I just want to get home."

Cliff shrugged. "We'll go back and pick up my car, then, and get you home."

* * * * *

A little over an hour later, Amy realized she had never been happier than right now, riding in the big, comfortable car beside her husband. Safe, secure. And on solid ground. Baby-soft leather caressed her legs, and the radio played a soft piano melody. The storm was raging in full strength by now, but Amy felt safe and warm. Peace reigned everywhere. They drove silently, Amy gazing into the blackness beyond the cozy confines of the car. The windshield wipers were sweeping back and forth in a furious, rhythmic frenzy.

She felt such relief when Cliff turned into their own

driveway. After a moment of silence while the garage door whirred open, Cliff drove into the three-car garage and cut the engine. Somehow, the safety and security of being home made the ordeal she had just gone through seem far away. She could still remember that suffocating blackness as she had waited helplessly, hoping against hope that friends would hurry and find her. Now that it was over, and the realization swept over her that she was truly alive, Amy felt herself trembling.

They sat there quietly in the car for a moment. Cliff's fingers gently traced the features of his wife's face, the small, delicately carved nose, the high cheekbones. "You sure were lucky," he whispered. Amy nodded gratefully. "It's amazing!" Cliff went on. "Of all the spots where you could have landed—among all those trees—you dove right into that brush area. That's what saved you; it buffeted the impact."

Cliff studied her for a long moment in the darkness before he spoke again. "What were you doing over near the quarries?" His voice was growing edgy.

"Oh, honey, it was awful! I've never flown in such a nightmare before. I guess I drifted off course. That, with the awful visibility, should explain why I couldn't spot the airport. . . . I'm sorry, Cliff," she said, wondering what, exactly, she was apologizing for. Why was she always apologizing to him?

"Well," he went on after a pause, "you really should have waited, don't you think? Why did you take off in a storm like that?"

That old feeling of oppression crept over her. "It was perfectly clear when I left Sacramento. And besides—I wanted to get home . . . Cliff, I've got to talk to you about Mama."

But he went on as though he had not heard her, pent-up worry and frustration dripping from his voice. "Why didn't you take the time to check the in-flight weather?"

"I—"

"Why didn't you take time to gas up? Why—"

"Cliff, I'm guilty, guilty! Now let's drop it." She already felt bad enough.

"We have to get this settled before the FAA—"

"Cliff," Amy said sharply. "I will not argue with you."

With that, she jumped out of the car. Wanting to see her kids, she burst through the door and into the kitchen, coming face to face with Bethany. "Mom!"

Two quick hugs and sloppy kisses later, they tumbled into the family room, followed by Cliff and Miriam.

"Mercy, Ms. Harper," Miriam said, "we've been hearing some scary things about you. Mr. Anderson said on the phone, you've been in a wreck."

"You crashed the plane, huh, Mom?"

Amy laughed, the soft sound drifting through the house with a welcoming tone. "I guess I did!"

Bethany was almost as tall as her mother, and her long, blond hair, full and rich, was tied back in a pony tail. Amy and Cliff had wondered where the girl had gotten her blond hair, since both of them were brunettes. She was dressed now in a soft, yellow, flannel nightgown that was trimmed with just a touch of lace. She planted her plump, young face close to Amy's. "Are you okay, Mom?"

"A little sore, and probably a couple of bruises. But

I was really lucky." Amy toppled onto the long leather couch in the family room. Her dark hair cascaded onto the back of the couch, the tresses having been arbitrarily loosed from their rubber band sometime during her ordeal. "I'm simply going to die, though," she said, casting a meaningful, plaintive look at Miriam, "if I don't get a cup of coffee." Miriam smiled, her dark eyes luminous with joy that her employer was safely at home. Without a word, she turned and headed into the kitchen.

"Where's Jen?"

Bethany made a face. "Out with Billy."

"Billy, huh?" Amy glanced at her husband, who was warming himself by the fireplace. The fire was going good and strong, and the crackling sounds made a warm and hearty welcome for the weary traveler. "Cliff, don't you think Jennifer's seeing too much of Billy?"

Cliff turned his body to face the fireplace. "We need to talk about that," he murmured. "Later."

"I get the hint," said Bethany, glancing at her wristwatch. "Wow, it's getting late. I need to get to bed." With that, she gave her mother a quick hug, turned, and disappeared down the softly carpeted hall to her room.

Amy turned a worried face to her husband. "So what's with Jennifer and Billy?"

"Probably nothing," he said with a frown. "They didn't come in last night until after two o'clock. Said they forgot the time."

"Forgot the time! That's not like Jennifer!" Amy started clicking her fingernails in that absent-minded, determined way she had. "And did they say what they had been doing that was so all-fired exciting that they forgot the time?"

Miriam came padding back into the room across the oval braided rug and set a large, brown ceramic mug of steaming liquid on the coffee table. Amy let out a squeal of delight. "Ooh, thank you, Miriam!"

Cliff eased down beside her, watching as she held the mug of coffee beneath her nose, deliciously enjoying the aroma. He allowed her a couple of long and luxurious sips before he answered. "They said they were playing miniature golf."

"Cliff, we need to do something about this right now."

"Maybe we can sit down with them tomorrow sometime. We'll get to the bottom of it. But now," Cliff said, heaving a huge, exaggerated sigh, "tell me about your trip. Did you get your story?"

"Yup."

"May I read it?"

"Not until it's finished. Most of it's on tape, anyway."

"You did get in—to the governor then?"

Amy laughed that crystal laugh of hers. "Of course I got in, and I got enough good grassroots stuff for an article on abortion rights that'll make the most vocal little prolifer tremble in her boots. They think they're so smart."

"Well, congratulations. Women's issues are important, too, I guess."

"You guess?"

"Honey, you know what I mean."

No, she didn't know what he meant, but she knew that if she pursued it, they would be into another fight. It seemed that the harder Amy worked for women's rights, the more he found fault with what she was doing. She had almost stopped doing marches and rallies, though, because the deeper she got involved in journalism, the more she had come to realize the power and might of the written word. Journalists had tremendous influence, and she felt she could contribute more by writing than by leading all the big rallies in the world. Recently, she had become one of the serious contenders for the current editor's vacancy at *She,* a regional feminist magazine with a wide and influential readership. She wanted that job so badly that she could almost taste it, and she refused to let Cliff hold her back or get her discouraged.

Amy was in her final semester at the university and would soon—ah, soon!—have her hard-earned bachelor's degree. She smiled now, remembering how some well-meaning friends had warned her against going back to school at her age. They had predicted that it would be too difficult and that she'd end up dropping out. Well, she had showed them all.

Amy curled her legs up underneath her. "I'm so keyed up," she said, "too keyed up to sleep." Her fingers began to trace little circles on Cliff's large hand. His wedding band fit tighter than when they were first married, and Amy noticed the paunch around his middle that had seemed to sprout sometime this past year.

They sat watching the fire as it began to die out. Memories of other times, other nights, went through Amy's mind, a time when love was fresh and new. Something was wrong with her and Cliff, and she couldn't put her finger on what it was. On the surface, everything looked good: a beautiful home, a good life, plenty of money, two good kids. But something was wrong, and it frightened Amy. The thought of losing Cliff was unbearable, something she would not let herself even contemplate.

And yet she knew that refusing to think about it would not make the problem go away. Somehow, on some level, Amy knew that the whole thing was getting ready to blow up.

4

Amy's Dilemma

A short while later, Amy sat at the dressing table, looking at herself in the mirror. "Cliff?" She had just dropped the bombshell and was waiting for his response. She gingerly patted the cut on her forearm with some witch hazel.

"It's not that I don't like your mother," Cliff was saying. "It's just that it would never work out, her living with us."

Amy stared at him in frustration. "But why not?"

"I don't mean to be unkind, Amy, but your mother is not a good influence on our family."

"How on earth can you say such a thing?"

Cliff shot his wife a look of exasperation. "You can't even get along with her yourself, and she's your mother."

"That's not true. We're both independent, and we clash sometimes. We agree to disagree. But I love my mom. We get along fine. You're the one who can't get along with her, Cliff. It's almost as if you—as if you've got it *in* for my mom."

"That's ridiculous, Amy; don't be silly."

"You know what I think, Cliff?" He raised an eyebrow. "I think you feel guilty around my mom because she's spiritual and you're not." He managed a laugh. "It's true," she went on. "You feel—what's the word?—convicted."

"It's all that spiritual stuff that causes the problems," said Cliff. "She tries to force her religion on me, cram it down my throat. She also tries to run everything every time she comes."

"You're crazy," Amy's eyes flashed with fire. "She doesn't force anything on anybody—not even on me, and I'm her daughter." Oh, it was hopeless. What was the use?

She glared at her husband, and she felt those old resentments rise up. She knew her mother better than anyone else. She realized the older woman could be a handful because her mind was full of energy and had a way of racing ahead of her body. She was almost eighty and had never really been sick in her life. Now she was sick and weak and dependent on others. She was an independent lady, not accustomed to being a burden to anyone.

Amy remembered how close her mother and father had been before he passed away two years ago. They did everything together, right up to the end. He died in the hospital, with Mom sitting there holding his hand and wiping his brow. He had said, "This is it, sweetheart," and then slipped away. Amy's eyes watered now as she remembered her dad. How she had loved him!

And now here was her mother. Alone and sick, and no one to take care of her. She had just lost everything she owned and loved and cherished in the whole world in that awful fire.

Amy really wished she had a brother or sister instead of having been an only child. It was just Amy, born in her mother's mid thirties. No other relatives; just a distant cousin back in South Carolina somewhere.

"I don't know what to do," lamented Amy. "There's no one to take care of her, nowhere for her to go when she leaves the hospital."

"What about a nursing home?"

"After all she's been through? Have a heart, Cliff—I couldn't do that to her."

Cliff shrugged. "What choice do you have?"

She whirled around to face him, her fiery eyes boring into his in an unbroken, unspoken challenge. "I'll figure something out," she promised. "No one is going to make me stick my mother in an old folks' home—and that includes you!" Then she reached over and clicked off the small crystal lamp on the dressing table, bathing the room in sudden blackness. Cliff rolled over in the bed, pulling the covers over his head. It took a moment for her eyes to adjust to the darkness, and then she slipped into bed beside her husband and adjusted the covers under her arms. Cliff was already fast asleep.

She lay there in the stillness, allowing herself the luxury of enjoying the thrill of being in her own bed. She had spent the last four nights on a rickety little hospital cot in her mother's room. During the days she had tried to balance spending time with her mother and running around the capital getting information for her article for *She* magazine.

Amy stretched out, the cool, crisp sheets caressing her legs. Her mind returned to thoughts of Jennifer. Lovely, smart, straight A's. She had been accepted at the university for this fall and would be pursuing a degree in political science. Jennifer had shone in this area all through high school. She was already working in the governor's race, getting an early start by knocking on doors and spending countless hours on the phone. Jennifer estimated that she had personally talked with over a thousand people already, extolling the virtues of her candidate.

Amy's thoughts continued to drift through memories of life with her family. It had been an ordinary life. They had lived in one city for the past fifteen years. Little Bethany had been born right here in Lawton, and Amy was such a settled homebody that she would probably never budge from Lawton.

She was so tired. Her body ached, and she found herself fighting to stay awake. Jennifer was still out, and Amy had never been able to go to sleep unless her children were tucked safely in their beds.

In spite of her intentions, Amy drifted off to sleep. She awoke with a start, the pale dawn light beginning to filter into the room. Just outside the window, early-morning birds were singing in perfect, harmonious unison. Gruff, the rooster, was announcing another day down at the barn. Cliff was snoring, in loud competition with the birds, and Amy slipped from the bed and down the hall to Jennifer's bedroom.

She quietly opened the door and peered inside. In the early-morning light, the bed lay in undisturbed peace. It had not been slept in, and Amy felt a chill go down her spine.

She raced through the house to the kitchen, only to find everything dark and quiet. Amy reached for the light switch on the kitchen wall, but something stopped her. A muffled sound. The outline of a solitary figure sitting at the darkened kitchen table. "Who's there?"

"It's me, ma'am."

"Miriam? What are you doing sitting here in the dark?"

"It's just my quiet time," the housekeeper responded. "Is something the matter, Ms. Harper?"

"Have you seen Jennifer?"

"Not since yesterday."

Amy spun around and rushed down the hall. Back in her room again, she started shaking her husband. "Cliff, wake up!"

"Uhhh."

"Cliff! Please! Jennifer's still not home."

Cliff rolled over and glared sleepily at the clock. Almost six-thirty. "Not home?"

"Cliff, call the police."

Cliff bolted upright and sprang out of bed, climbing into his robe as he made his way down the hall. After seeing for himself that his wife was not having a bad dream, he headed for the phone and notifed the police.

"What do you mean, twenty-four hours?" Cliff shouted into the telephone.

"What's all the ruckus?" asked Bethany, coming into the kitchen, still rubbing her eyes. She slipped into a seat at the kitchen table, her large, blue eyes curious.

"Jennifer didn't come home last night," said Amy.

Cliff slammed the phone down with a loud clatter. "I don't believe this," he said. "Wait twenty-four hours. A person could be *dead* by then."

"Cliff, please."

Miriam had put the coffee on and was serving everyone a cup before she started breakfast.

"You know what they're thinking, don't you? They're thinking Jennifer ran off with her boyfriend."

"Is that what they said?"

"Not in so many words, but that's what they're thinking."

"Jennifer ran away?" asked Bethany, a look of horror on her face.

Amy placed her hand over her daughter's plump young ones. "No, dear, your sister did not run away."

"Then where is she, Mother?"

Amy just stared blindly at the coffee cup. She had no answers.

5

New Directions

The twenty-four hours had not yet passed, and there was still no sign of Jennifer. Cliff was nervous and angry, having to wait while the hands of the clock ticked past, doing nothing. A pall of gloom had settled over the Harper household. Cliff bristled under the police suspicion that his daughter had run away.

But had she? The funny thing was that Billy Eversole was also missing. The thought of Jennifer and Billy running away together infuriated Cliff. Not only did it upset him that his daughter might fall for a ranch hand, but it angered him that a ranch hand would have the audacity to steal his little girl. A fine man, Billy. He really was. He had a lot of good qualities. But he had been married and divorced and was almost thirty. And Jennifer? She had always been so mature and levelheaded. Only childish brats or juvenile delinquents ran away from home. Not girls like Jennifer.

Cliff Harper sat at his mammoth desk now, his back

turned toward the center of his office. He was gazing out the window at Lawton's skyline. It was a crisp, sunny day, and a slight haze was creeping over the horizon. His eyes wandered over to the northeasterly edge of town toward the huge piece of land his company had just acquired. Cliff was excited about it. He had made connections with a non-profit organization that wanted to build a maternity home on the land. Actually, it was more like a ranch. It had forty acres of spacious room to be used by the young women as they learned skills such as gardening and carpentry and husbandry. They also planned to have several acres just for animals.

The executive director, Lorene Fields, worked out of her agency's office in New Orleans, Louisiana. She had explained to Cliff, "Working with animals is tremendous therapy. It is especially good for girls like these, girls who are feeling unloved and rejected."

"How so?" Cliff wanted to know.

"Animals just have a way," she said, "of making you feel loved. They accept you just as you are. They are loyal, dedicated. They make good friends."

"I see," said Cliff, impressed with the plans for his ranch. Cliff had gotten involved initially because of tax advantages, but the more he heard about the work of the organization, Mothers' Ark, the more gratified he felt by being involved.

"Carpentry is very creative," the director went on. "The girls will learn to build items, not only for their own homes when they leave, but also for use around the ranch. They will feel useful. And gardening. Great therapy. There's just something about working in God's earth. It's almost like depositing all our ills and negative feelings right into the dirt and burying them there. It's getting close to nature, close to creation."

"Where do these girls come from?" asked Cliff. He enjoyed watching the fire of excitement dance in Lorene's eyes as she talked about her project.

"From all over. We plan to advertise nationally, and we will be hooked up with all the adoption and prolife agencies. We already have a toll-free hotline."

"How large a place do you envision?" asked Cliff. "How many girls?"

"At first, we plan to have a facility to house twenty. We've built in several expansion phases for development as time goes by."

"Well," said Cliff, "count me in. I think something like this is really needed."

The director had looked at him long and hard. "Do you really?" she asked. "Most people aren't enthusiastic about unmarried pregnant women."

Cliff's face burrowed in a frown. Too bad, he thought now, that they weren't building a ranch for old people. Then Granny Dix would have a place to stay. He just couldn't stand the thought of living with her! They clashed too much, and it seemed as if she read his mind all the time. She would look at him with those cool, gray eyes, and Cliff got the uncanny feeling she knew everything he had ever done or thought. It was creepy.

Cliff swiveled in his chair now as he remembered that discussion with Lorene. Lorene. Tall and dramatically dark, she reminded Cliff of a Greek movie star he had once seen in a film. The star had been sunning on a yacht, enjoying the pleasures of life on an exotic Grecian island. Cliff wondered what Lorene did for pleasure when she wasn't working. He didn't have a yacht, but he did have a mighty comfortable cabin cruiser.

Cliff mentally kicked himself for being so lazy today and letting his mind wander. And he knew he should stop these fantasies about Lorene. He leaned back in his leather chair, resting his head against the high back. His desk was a large one, solid oak, and a brass eagle with wings spread wide in flight rested near the desk's right edge. Cliff liked eagles. They represented power, and with enough power, one could accomplish great things. The carpeting was cream colored, like the heavy draperies, very elegantly coordinated with the oak and brass. But other than a matching credenza and two chairs, the rest of the mammoth office was sparse. Very simple.

Simplicity was the image Cliff strived for, and to those who did not know him well, he did seem uncomplicated. But to those who were close to him, Cliff Harper was an enigma, a paradox. With a country background, he was a self-made man. His command of the English language was basic and elementary. He knew no foreign languages. He met people on their own level and felt at home among the rich and poor alike. But while seemingly open and transparent, Cliff Harper was a very private person. Not even his own wife knew how private.

The ringing of the phone awakened Cliff from his reverie. The lighted button indicated that the call was coming through on his private line.

It was Amy. "Cliff, you heard anything from Jennifer?"

"No. I was hoping you had."

"I wish. . . . But I do have some good news."

"Well, I'd love to hear something good."

A brief silence. "I got the job!"

"The job? At *She?*"

A little squeal. "Yup! Oh, Cliff, I'm so happy! I'm doing little dance steps all around the kitchen."

Cliff laughed. He could see her now, her lean body doing little pirouettes across the shiny, white tiles. Cliff felt a wave of pride wash over him. Although he felt threatened by his wife's talents and intelligence, he was also proud of her. But the very intelligence he so much admired was also intimidating. He had always been glad she was his. What was different now?

"Cliff?"

"Yes?"

"I feel guilty for being so happy, what with Jennifer gone and all."

"Life has to go on, Amy."

"I was on the verge of getting good and drunk," Amy said, "when I got the news. I'm actually an editor! And not just any kind of editor, but one in a position to really be of benefit to women."

"Well," he said, "congratulations."

"Let's celebrate after work?"

"Gee, I'm sorry, honey. If I'd known a little earlier . . ."

Cliff could tell she was disappointed, but he couldn't cancel his appointment tonight. It was dinner with Lorene Fields, who was flying all the way out from New Orleans. The Mothers' Ark project was too important; Cliff just couldn't cancel out now.

"Well," said Amy, "we can do it later. Or maybe I can join you in whatever it is you're doing tonight?"

"We'll do something special this weekend. I promise."

After a brief silence, Amy asked, "It's Lorene Fields again, isn't it?"

Cliff was immediately defensive and could not understand why. "Amy," he said slowly, with a great show of patience, "this is an important deal. Lorene is the one who heads it up. That's all there is to it."

Amy bristled. "You are seeing too much of her, Cliff."

"It's not like you to be jealous."

"I don't mean to sound jealous."

"Then don't."

"There's something not right about her."

"Amy . . ."

"Keep your eyes open, Cliff. I'd hate to see you get messed up. I have a gut feeling about this."

"Goodbye, Amy."

6

Prodigal Children

Cliff came home that night just shortly after midnight. Amy was perched at the kitchen bar, drinking from a pot of freshly made coffee. "Hi, hon," he said, coming directly into the kitchen from the garage. He started to say something else, but the look on her face stopped him cold. "What's wrong?"

Amy just continued to sit there on the bar stool, her face ashen. She felt like spitting on him for coming in so jauntily from his evening with the famous Miss Fields. Instead, she said, "Your daughter's home."

"*My* daughter?" Cliff's eyes darted around excitedly, and he made a move to take off down the hall.

"Wait, Cliff."

"Do you want to tell me what's going on or not?" he demanded. "Is she okay?"

"I'm more than okay, Daddy, I'm fantastic." That was Jennifer, appearing in the doorway. Directly behind her towered Billy, their fingers interlocked. Cliff poured him self a cup of coffee, more to keep his hands busy than anything else.

They all stood in awkward silence for a moment. Finally Amy spoke. "Well, do you want to tell your father what's going on?"

Cliff was startled at the sharp, impatient sound in his wife's voice. He could not tolerate this suspense any longer. "Let's all sit down."

Everyone filed behind him into the family room, Jennifer and Billy huddling together on the couch. Cliff scowled at his hired hand, but it was Jennifer who spoke. "Daddy. We—we're married."

"Married?" Cliff set his coffee mug down so hard that some of its contents sloshed out.

"I'm sorry—we're both sorry—that we felt we had to run away to do it."

"But why, babe? I don't understand."

So the police had been right after all: a runaway. Cliff was embarrassed at the way he had flown off the handle with the police. They were only doing their job, and they obviously knew more about these matters than he did. Cliff felt a wave of anger in spite of his efforts to remain calm and compassionate. "Didn't you know we'd be worried sick?"

Amy's fingernails were drumming rhythmically on the kitchen counter.

"Oh, Daddy, I'm sorry. I just didn't even think about something like that. At least not at first. We were just so happy."

"I don't understand. Are you pregnant?"

"Daddy! That's not fair!"

Cliff flushed and shot an embarrassed look at Amy.

"Say what you have to, Daddy. We know we did wrong to run away like that, went about it the wrong way. We apologize." Amy and Cliff both visibly relaxed. "But please, be happy for me. I love Billy so much."

"And I love your daughter," interjected Billy. "I cherish her."

Jennifer turned and looked at her new husband with eyes that glittered. Happiness exuded from both of them, and in the face of it, it was difficult not to share in their joy. Clinging to her new husband's hand, Jennifer went on, "We knew you wouldn't agree to it, and I always thought the way that you two got married—eloping like this—was *so* utterly romantic." Cliff and Amy exchanged a quick, embarrassed look. "So we just did it." Jennifer's lovely, liquid eyes searched her mother's imploringly. "Mom, Dad . . . please understand."

"What about college?"

Jennifer squirmed against the leather. "What about it?"

"Have you changed your mind about college?"

"No. I still want to go. Except we'll probably be moving to Sacramento, so I'd like to go to State. Billy will be going to State. I'd like to go along with him."

Cliff's eyes brightened. "You're going to college, Billy?"

"I'd like to give it a try, yes."

"I never thought I'd see the day. . . . Well, I'm glad to hear that, son."

Billy appeared to relax at the form of address and went on, "They've got a good business program, and with two of us in school, money's going to be tight. We've talked it through; it should work out all right."

"Forgive me, Billy," said Cliff, "but I don't recall ever seeing you in a business suit. It's hard to picture."

"Well, I guess I can learn. I want to be a good provider for my family, and I can earn more in business than as a cowboy."

Amy smiled, warming to this new facet of their relationship. Cliff rubbed his hands together. "Well now, it's late. We'd better be getting on to bed." As he stood up, he held out a hand to Billy. "Well, son," he beamed, "welcome to the family. I wish you had waited, but since you didn't—well, welcome, anyhow."

* * * * *

Amy sat at the bar in the kitchen long after the family had gone to sleep. She had brewed another pot of coffee, her third one tonight, and now it too was almost empty. She was torn in so many pieces that she didn't know how to begin to put them all together. Jennifer's unspoken accusation hurt. Amy had never thought eloping with Cliff was "romantic." It was simply a necessary fact of life. Even though she adored him, she had *had* to marry him. Back in those days, eloping was common when a girl became pregnant.

There was a big scene at home, Amy remembered now. Her parents were so disappointed. All of that, only to end up not having the baby after all. But she and Cliff had married, and divorce was something most people just didn't think of. At least not back then.

That was a long time ago, brooded Amy. And now it was coming back to haunt her and rob her own daughter of a lovely church wedding. Romantic, indeed. If only kids would just stop and think!

Well, Amy would just shut down her mind and refuse to think. With grim determination, she shut off the lights and doggedly made her way to bed. Somehow, it would all work out.

7

Welcome, Granny Dix!

To Jennifer, Billy's little cabin had looked like honeymoon heaven, and they had moved into it right away. Jennifer had plunged into scrubbing and sewing and hanging lovely lady things on the walls. She had tried her hand at cooking, but after only two days, Billy had tired of imaginative delicacies like green eggs and purple rice, and the couple resumed taking their meals at Miriam's hand.

Then, when they had been living in the little one-room structure for a week, one of the local pets, an oversized field rat, persuaded Jennifer to take up residence in her old bedroom. It had been different, having Billy living in the Harper household. It was one of those make-do situations, since they would soon be leaving Lawton anyway for the capital, and Jennifer relegated most of the domestic duties to the future somewhere.

Tonight was one of those rare evenings that Cliff was home, and the family was sitting outside on the patio after dinner. Cliff was scanning his news journal in the twilight, and Amy rested, eyes half closed, in a chaise lounge. Early spring had ushered in fields of flowers—colorful, cheery, and filling the air with soft and fragrant scents. Billy and Jennifer sat in the swing, gently squeaking back and forth. Suddenly Jennifer sat straight up. "Oh, Mom, I forgot to tell you! The hospital called today and said they have to know where to send Granny Dix. You need to call them, they said, first thing tomorrow."

"Thanks, dear."

Jennifer rushed on. "It'll be fun, won't it, having her here with us?"

Cliff looked up from his paper, peering over his little executive reading glasses. "She will not be staying here," he said. "Your mother and I have already settled that."

Jennifer looked dismayed. "Mom!"

"Don't look at me; that's your father's decision."

"What is going on around here?" demanded Jennifer. Her eyes searched the faces of her parents for some clue as to the answer to this awful riddle.

Amy took the last sip of her lemonade and set the glass down on the little wrought-iron table beside her chair. "What's going on," she said, "is that your father feels Granny Dix does not belong here but in a nursing home instead."

Jennifer stared at Cliff, her mouth slightly open. "Daddy!"

"What?"

"You know it's not right to just toss Granny Dix out to the wolves."

"It's hardly tossing her to the wolves, honey. This Rest Haven Home is quite expensive, and she'll get the best of everything there. It's luxurious, and it also has many of the little touches of home."

Bethany, who had been sitting on the ground with her head on Amy's lap, piped in. "Rest Haven? Sounds like a graveyard."

"Daddy, please no!"

Amy leaned back in her chair, determined to stay out of this. She had already made up her mind that she would take care of her mother one way or another, so she was just biding her time. She sat there listening as though this family belonged to someone she had only just read about in a book somewhere. Maybe even on TV, on one of those soap operas she had heard so much about.

"Jen," Cliff said patiently, "where do you propose we put your grandmother? There's not enough room."

"Not enough room? This place is huge; there's plenty of room."

"Land, maybe. And recreational room. But there are no extra bedrooms."

"She can have my room."

"And where will you live?"

Jennifer's shoulders squared in a valiant gesture. "Billy and I will move into the cabin, right, Billy? See— it's all settled."

"And the rats?"

Jennifer grimaced. "It'll work out."

Cliff looked at his daughter there in the darkening night. Her firm, young chin was held high in that determined way she had. Her mind was set. There would be no changing it. His heart sank. He would give that girl the moon if he could.

"Well," he finally said, "it seems as if the women in this family outnumber me."

"Does that mean you'll give in?"

Cliff sighed. It would be easier giving her the moon. "I guess I have to," he said. "I guess we'll have to let your grandmother stay with us for a while. But it's only until she gets on her feet again."

With his pronouncement, Jennifer dove at him, encircling him in her arms. "Oh, Daddy, thank you! You'll never be sorry; wait and see."

* * * * *

But Cliff was sorry. The day he saw Granny Dix shuffling up the makeshift ramp to the front door, he was sorry. But he purposed in his heart to be kind to her, at least for the girls' sake. Amy had an important interview on the day Granny Dix was to come home from the hospital, so the girls had driven to Sacramento to pick her up. They had packed a lunch and a gallon of fresh sun tea and decided to make a holiday of it.

The older woman had adamantly refused to set foot inside an airplane, and Amy had balked at the thought of driving that distance. Which reminded Cliff: she was balking at flying again, period. She used the excuse of waiting until her own Cessna was repaired, but Cliff worried that it was fear. It was very important after a crash to get behind the controls again right away. Fear could keep one from ever flying again. And Amy was one of those people who needed to fly—it was part of her, it was in her blood.

Cliff watched silently as the three figures made their way to the front door. Jennifer was on one side of her grandmother, and Bethany on the other. The girls were laughing, and it was obvious that Granny Dix was enjoying herself. What on earth could such a pitiable creature find to enjoy? Cliff wondered. Surely she must understand that her life was over.

There was that ugly sack she always carried with her, the thing she called her ditty-bag. She kept everything in that beat-up old vinyl bag, and it was bulging at its seams. Now it was slung over one arm, dangling at an awkward angle. Cliff once remarked in front of his mother-in-law that he would like to start a garden in the space behind the house. Immediately, she began rummaging through her ditty-bag, retrieved two packages of carrot seeds, and proudly presented them to him as her contribution to the family garden. Another time, to Cliff's dismay, she had withdrawn a set of battery cables, even though she didn't even own an automobile. That bag, thought Cliff, could be dangerous.

As he watched sullenly through the front window, Cliff saw the woman throw her head back and give a big belly laugh. "You girls work a body to death," that soft southern voice sang out. "You're killing me."

"C'mon, Granny Dix," Jennifer was encouraging, "you can make it. Just a few more steps."

"If you think I'm not hurrying," she kidded the girls, "you got another thought coming. Now just get out of my way and watch my dust."

Cliff was disgusted. What dust? An eighty-year-old woman can't kick up any dust. But part of Cliff hurt inside, too, seeing the changes in his mother-in-law. In the year since he had last seen her, she had aged a lot. Cliff remembered her being taller, straighter somehow, and moving much faster. She must have lost at least thirty pounds, and her old skin hung in folds. Grief takes its toll, he mused, sometimes harder than age.

Granny Dix finally made it into the house and settled on the sofa. There she was, plumping the soft, rose-colored pillows all around her and getting comfortable. She looked strikingly female for one so old, Cliff thought. His eyes took in her apparel, a simple, faded, housedress, pale rose. Simple house shoes, worn and frayed. Simple hair, pulled back in a little yellow-white bun near the nape of her neck. Granny Dix had once had hair so long it reached down to her knees, but most of it had since fallen out. Simple lady. No lace or ribbons or satin, yet she looked strangely feminine.

"And, Cliff dear, how are you?" Granny Dix's voice was as soft as Cliff always remembered it. Soft and lilting, it was the one thing Cliff had always enjoyed about his mother-in-law.

"I'm fine, Granny Dix," he answered, looking into the deep, gray eyes. She peered back through her little rim glasses. The left lens was broken, a jagged crack right down the center of it. The glasses perched precariously across the bridge of her nose as though they might topple off if she moved too suddenly. Cliff wondered how she could see through all the smudges and grimy fingerprints. "Well, Granny Dix, welcome to our home—*your* home now."

"Thank you, son." She struggled to get into a comfortable position. "It was awfully kind of you to take me in. I do appreciate it."

Cliff knew this must be difficult for her. Surely this woman must be hurting, having everything taken away from her. He remembered the home she had just lost to fire. He had picked Amy up for their first date in that home. There were many memories there. A lovely, white, wooden house with green trim, and a soft, green lawn laced with all kinds of flowers. Zinnias, azaleas, thrift. . . . Late summer evenings were always fragrant as he and Amy sat together in the swing on the wide front porch. The house had stayed lovely over the years, always fresh and neat. It was a terrible loss to have it consumed by flames. He felt a stab of pity. "It must be awfully hard," he said, "losing everything."

Granny Dix looked at him long and soberly. "The Lord giveth, son, and the Lord taketh away. He knows all about it."

"Well." Cliff fidgeted in the chair. "Well, make yourself at home," he said. "I believe the girls took your luggage to Jennifer's old room."

"Good. I'll turn in for a nap shortly," she said. "You realize, of course, that this is only a temporary situation until I can get back on my feet."

"Of course."

Cliff clasped his hands, rubbing them together. He suppressed the twinge of pity that rose up in his heart. He would not let this woman get to him! If he weakened toward her, he would be weakening toward her God, and that would ruin everything. "Well, Amy should be getting home any minute now."

* * * * *

After Granny Dix closed the door to her new room, she lay down stiffly on the bed. She found herself sorely missing her own bed back home. It was hard to realize that she would never see her room again, never smell the flowers as they bloomed and blossomed in the garden outside her bedroom window. Somehow, in a way, it all seemed so unreal.

The days in the hospital had been acutely lonesome, filled as they were with pain and uncertainty. But somehow, today the lonesomeness in her heart transcended all of that. She missed her home so dreadfully. And it seemed like yesterday, not two years ago, that she first became a widow. The loss still cut deeply into her soul because not only did she miss her Jack, but she knew he had not been saved. Oh, God, that was the deepest hurt of all.

Finally, Dixie felt herself relaxing. This is a lovely room, she thought, her eyes slowly beginning to take it all in. It smelled like Jennifer, airy, light, with a touch of rose. Jennifer had lived and spun dreams and grown up in this room with the pink satin curtains. Granny Dix felt she was floating on a pink cloud in a pink sky. Everything was pink. But it didn't bother Granny Dix one bit. She enjoyed the feeling of Jennifer, her first grandchild. Very special, she was, the apple of her grandma's eye.

Dixie heard an echo in the halls of her memory, an echo of the words of an excited two-year-old Jennifer: "Granny Dix, Granny Dix!" Granny Dix had hooted as the toddler tumbled over her words. The little girl found "Grandmother Dixie" too cumbersome to say, so she shortened it to Granny Dix. And Granny Dix it had remained.

Just as she felt herself drifting off to sleep, she thought of Cliff. She had tried with all her heart to be his friend but had never discovered the secret. It hurt now to know that he did not want her here. But Dixie was not one to give in to self-pity, and even as a monstrous tear cascaded down her cheek, her face lit up with the glory of the Lord. She gave herself to thoughts of Him, knowing she would need His strength in the days to come. She told herself that the worst was behind her. Granny Dix had no way of knowing the nightmare that was yet to come.

* * * * *

Miriam put the last of the pot roast onto the table. "Can I get you something else?"

Amy's eyes surveyed the perfectly set table, the fresh-cut flowers, the elegant china and crystal. "No, thank you, Miriam; everything is lovely."

Granny Dix was having her first meal in her new home. While the others started eating right away, she unobtrusively closed her eyes and gave thanks to her Lord. She had a lot to be thankful for: recovery, a new home, a nice dinner prepared by able, compassionate hands, a daughter and son-in-law, and two lovely grand-daughters who doted on her. And tonight she had finally gotten to meet this Billy who had married her Jennifer.

He was a nice young man, Granny Dix could tell. Ah yes, there was much to give thanks for. She swallowed the large lump that homesickness had lodged in her throat. Better not to think about what used to be, and what could have been. The tired old eyes glistened with an unshed tear, and she turned her attention to her little family.

Amy was dishing a huge chunk of meat onto her mother's plate. The only thing was, Granny Dix could not eat it. Her teeth were too bad, what was left of them, and try as she might, she was never able to chew meat in public. The only way she could chew meat was to remove her partial and just gum it, as they say. But that always left a glaring cavern right in the front of her mouth, which had a way of frightening people, and Granny Dix did not want to frighten her family. So she picked up a piece of bread, smeared it with butter, and nibbled at it. That should tide her over until she could sneak back in for a snack later, after everyone went to bed.

"Mother, you aren't eating."

"Don't want to."

"Mother, you have to eat. You must keep up your strength."

Granny Dix looked at her daughter for a moment. "If you insist," she said, reaching into her mouth and pulling out her teeth. Resisting the temptation to plunk them into her water glass, she rolled them up in the napkin and set the little package beside her plate. Her arthritis prevented her from using a knife the way she would like, so she began pulling the roast apart with her remaining teeth and proceeded to chew the meat, as best she could, with great gusto.

Bethany stared, her eyes large and round, her mouth ajar. Billy dropped his fork.

Jennifer, with great aplomb, reached over and began to cut the roast into bite-sized pieces. "Where's Dad?" she asked, to change the subject. "He was here earlier; isn't he coming to the table?"

"Your father went out," Amy said stiffly.

"Again?" Jennifer and Billy exchanged a look.

Granny Dix averted her eyes, absorbed in pushing a potato around on her plate. It felt as if there were a brick in her stomach, a deep ache. She wished it were bedtime.

8

New Pressures

Somehow, in spite of all the pressures and absurdities overwhelming her life, Amy made it through till graduation.

It was Friday afternoon. Hot and steamy, she stood with the rest of her graduating class at the back of the huge auditorium, giggling with them just as though she were as young as they were. Her heart tingled with excitement as she anticipated seeing all her family inside. They would be there, all of them, somewhere in the throng of people. It was very humbling, Amy thought, just knowing how proud they were of her. It humbled her and encouraged her to always do her very best.

College graduation at her age. In her heart she felt that if she could do it, others could do it. Her heart went out to those women who felt inferior and inadequate, women who felt the world had passed them by. Amy Harper determined to write to these women with the message that they are never too old to start school. There are really no limits to what a woman can accomplish, she would write, other than those mental and emotional limitations they place upon themselves.

The building was filled with the hum of restless, excited chatter, and—there it was! "Pomp and Circumstance!" Off they went down the aisle and through the sea of blurred faces, gathering into the rows of seats at the very front of the auditorium.

Amy held her head high, tears brimming her eyes. It was hot and stuffy, but she didn't mind. The invocation and the speeches were wonderful, but she hardly heard a word. They were talking about youthful visions for kids with long, productive years ahead. Amy left those dreams and visions for the rest of her class. They didn't apply to her. Not really. She had already had her share of them.

Then it was time to begin the long roll call, and she heard those magic words: "Amy May Harper." And when she marched up the steps and onto the platform there waited the president and the dean, and after a brief handshake, she resumed her place with the rest of her class. A new graduate! Now, she thought, she could get on with the business of living. But she would have to hurry. Tonight they would go through the same ceremonies for Jennifer over at the high school.

* * * * *

The next Monday morning Amy took the elevator up to the sixth floor of the Sussex Building. She stepped off the elevator, sinking into the deep, luxurious, blue carpeting. Even though she had been *She* editor a few weeks now, she was still apprehensive about her new job. What if, under her leadership, the magazine folded? What if they were sued and got into all kinds of legal trouble? What if they lost all their advertisers or, worse, all their readers? Amy felt as if she should turn in her resignation now, today, before she failed. That way, she could at least walk away with dignity.

Before she could pursue the idea further, the glass door to the offices of *She* magazine burst open, and out tumbled Skip Turner, account executive. "Hi, Amy, bye, Amy, gotta run." And off he raced, leaving Amy spinning in his dust.

She turned her head toward the melodious sound of laughter. Her secretary, Barbara, seemed to find the scenario funny. "Good morning, Amy," she said. "You get lost in the whirlwind?" Amy returned the laughter. It felt good to break the tension. "He's got an appointment in ten minutes," Barbara explained, "with Camden Company."

Amy pursed her lips in admiration. "The Camden Company, eh? That would certainly be a plum account."

"You know, our advertising revenue has doubled since Skip came on board six months ago."

"He knows his stuff." With that, Amy moved past Barbara and down the hall to her office. The walls were decorated with a soft paisley wallpaper, the deep rose carpet picking out shades of rose in the paper. In the center of the room was a white French provincial desk trimmed with gold. Large pictures of French Riviera scenery graced the walls, along with an authentic travel poster bearing a modernistic photograph of the Eiffel Tower. Some of Amy's happiest memories were of her and Cliff in Paris during one of his earlier business trips there. They had held hands atop the Eiffel Tower and had drifted down the Seine River beneath stars that winked in a coquettish Parisian way. A flush crept over Amy's face as she remembered the hilarious time when she and Cliff had changed clothes inside a cramped little European car— parked right on the busy Avenue Champs-Elysees! All of that had been long ago, Amy lamented, and now it seemed so far away. The deep pain of the sense of loss gripped at her heart.

She crossed over to the huge plate-glass window and looked out over the city. Amy loved the view. She could see the Camden River, right over there, as it wove its way through the western part of the town. Its banks were deserted now, but by lunch time they would be littered with people munching from brown bags, topping off their lunches with the funny little delicacies from the musical ice-cream carts.

Amy turned back to her desk. That's when she noticed the huge fuchsia plume.

"That's a gift for you," chirped Barbara, as though she had read her new boss's thoughts. "One of your writers brought it by. There's a card. Look," the secretary said, picking up the plume. "It's really a ballpoint pen in disguise."

"How clever." Amy turned the pen around in her fingers and then stuck it over her left ear like a giant feather. "Ole!"

The two women laughed heartily. "I'm glad you're

on board, Amy—you're a riot."

"Why, thank you, Barbara. It takes one to know one, you know." And they started laughing again. "We'll get along just fine. We'll make this magazine the best in the whole Wild West!"

But Amy wasn't as sure as her confident demeanor projected. What am I doing here? she wondered. What is a nobody like me doing, thinking she can run a magazine like this?

* * * * *

Shortly before lunch, Jay Gilt was waiting in the reception room for Amy. She was trying to get a subscriber off the line because she didn't want to keep the president of the board waiting. Finally, Barbara ushered him into Amy's office, and he ambled over to one of the delicate little chairs. Without a word, he plopped his large, solid frame into the chair. Amy noticed he was handsome in a rough sort of way, and he reminded her more of a rodeo rider than a corporation lawyer.

"Settling in okay?" his deep voice boomed.

"Just fine, thank you," said Amy.

Gilt's eyes were roving around the office, taking in the furnishings. "You got all new stuff?"

Suddenly Amy felt guilty, and her face flushed slightly. But her voice answered firmly. "There was money in the budget for it, so I did get a few new pieces, yes. But most of this was already here."

Amy did not know how to interpret his smile. "I would not expect a feminist to have dainty, ladylike furniture like this."

"Oh? Why not?"

Jay Gilt shrugged his large shoulders. "Never mind." He swooped one large hand into the little portfolio that had been balancing on his crossed knees. "Got a little piece here I'd like you to print in the first available issue."

Amy raised an eyebrow. "Oh?"

"That is, if you find it suitable, of course."

Amy reached for the manuscript. The title jumped out at her in bold dark letters: "The Right to Die with Great Dignity, by Jay E. Gilt."

"Mr. Gilt, is this article about what the title suggests it is about?"

"Of course."

Amy's eyes scanned the manuscript. She was a rapid reader and could get the gist of a piece very quickly. She said, "I really don't think it's suitable for *She*, do you?"

Jay Gilt uncrossed his long, limber legs and leaned back in the tiny, fragile chair. "My wife thought it was good. In fact, she's the one who suggested I bring it to you."

Amy sensed his disappointment. As a writer herself, she knew how sensitive writers could be about their work. She did not want to hurt this man. "Mr. Gilt, I'm not saying your article is not good. But *She* is a magazine written by feminists for feminists, and we're very upbeat. You know that. This isn't quite what I'm looking for."

"You surprise me."

"How's that?"

"You say you're a magazine for feminists, yet you don't seem to care about women's rights."

Amy blinked. "I'm afraid I don't follow you."

"Oh, never mind," he said, looking at his watch. The electric clock hanging on the wall was giving off its peculiar buzzing sound. "Well, will you at least do me the courtesy of thinking about it?"

Amy smiled softly. "Of course."

* * * * *

Barbara stared at her new boss in horror. "You actually turned him down?"

Amy was confused. "Of course. Why shouldn't I? An article on death is hardly what our upbeat readers want to read about. They're interested in how to have a better life."

"I know, but . . ."

"But what?"

Barbara was sitting in the same little chair that Jay Gilt had just vacated. After he briskly passed her desk, she had made a beeline for Amy's office. "People don't talk that way to Mr. Gilt."

"What way? All I did was turn down his article. That's an editor's prerogative."

"Yes but . . . the other editors always printed whatever he brought in—except Suzie, of course."

Amy was puzzled. "What other kinds of things have we printed by Mr. Gilt?"

"Mostly that death stuff. Didn't you ever read any of it?"

"Frankly, no. I usually skip over what looks boring and move on. And it's only been this past year that I've really sat down and made a study of the magazine."

"I don't think we printed any of his stuff this year. That's when Sue was here."

Amy made a face. "He's a lawyer; wonder why he's so interested in death?" Then: "You just said something about Suzie not printing his articles."

"Right. She turned him down. She felt like you do."

"What happened to her, anyway?"

Barbara sank back as far as she possibly could, considering the delicate chair. "Gilt got her fired."

* * * * *

Amy had been back from lunch about fifteen minutes when Miriam called. "Ms. Harper," she puffed into the phone, "Granny Dix is missing."

"Missing? What do you mean, missing?"

"Well, first, she didn't want any breakfast, just went for a nap. She came out of her room in about an hour and was heading to the patio." Amy was drumming her fingers, gripping what patience she had with all her might. It took Miriam so long to tell something! "She came and got a glass of iced tea out of the kitchen and was taking the glass with her and a book, I guess to read. She was headed for the patio. But I haven't seen her since."

"She can't have just disappeared."

"No, ma'am."

"I'll be home as quick as I can."

"Yes, ma'am."

Amy made the usual one-hour drive in thirty-five minutes. As she zipped up the driveway, Miriam was waiting for her in the front yard. "She's home, Ms. Harper, and she's fine!"

"Thank goodness. Where is she, Miriam?"

"On the patio."

Amy looked at the housekeeper sharply. "She was there all the time?"

"Oh no, ma'am. Right after hanging up talking to you I got a call from Mr. Pherson—over on the next ranch."

"Go on."

"Evidently, Granny Dix had wandered over there."

"Wandered over there?"

"Yes ma'am. She was just walking through his pasture, carrying her glass of iced tea and her book. It was really not a safe thing to do, Mr. Pherson said, because of all the cows."

"I reckon so." Amy felt like crying. What was happening to her mom?

"I called you back, Ms. Harper, but you had already left. I'm sorry you had to come all the way home for nothing."

"Never mind; it's okay. I think I'll take a glass of that iced tea before I head back to the office."

She was still trembling when she joined Granny Dix on the patio. "Mother, shame on you. Why did you go off like that?"

"Like what, dear?"

"You know. Over to the Pherson place."

Granny Dix's clear, gray eyes searched Amy's, a look of confusion welling up in them. "I really don't know what you mean, Amy."

"Mother, please."

With no warning, Granny Dix burst into tears. "I'm trying to help, Amy, but I don't know what you want of me!"

Amy was stunned. The times she had seen her mother cry had been so rare that it was startling now. She reached out and gathered her mother's two thin hands between her own and rubbed them gently. "Don't cry, Mother; everything's all right. Don't cry."

Amy left as soon as she could, stopped by her room, and had herself a good cry. What was happening to her mother? There seemed to be something different about her today, something that frightened Amy. She shuddered and began to pull herself together.

On the way out she asked Miriam, "There's no need to mention this to Mr. Harper, you understand, Miriam?"

"Mention what, Ms. Harper?" The two women exchanged a look of understanding.

Grateful, Amy returned to work.

She did not make it back to her desk. As soon as she walked in the front door, Barbara said, "I've been trying to reach you, Amy. You're needed at the hospital."

"Hospital?"

"Right away. It's Granny Dix."

9

Into the Shadows

Not being able to garner any more information, Amy turned around and headed to the hospital. There she found her mother in intensive care. Dr. Dean Wilson was her attending physician.

Amy had always liked Dr. Wilson. He was in his late sixties, had gray hair, and had a kind, compassionate manner. His eyes reflected a kindness and a wisdom that the ordinary person could never know. Although he moved slowly and deliberately, Dr. Wilson accomplished more in just a few minutes than others could do in an hour. There were many doctors in the world, Amy thought, but few real physicians. Dr. Wilson was a real physician. Professional, dedicated, principled.

Amy perched on a little, hard chair outside her mother's room, waiting for Dr. Wilson. The corridors were sparkling clean, with hospital personnel busily going to and fro, back and forth. Amy sat numbly.

"Hello, Amy."

She stood. "Dr. Wilson. How's my mother?"

He motioned for her to sit down, and he sat in the chair beside her. A slight frown crossing his brow, he said, "It's too early to tell, Amy. She's had what we suspect to be a cerebral vascular stroke. We're running some tests now to determine just what's going on."

Just looking into his soft, caring eyes made Amy want to cry. She struggled for control. "May I see her?"

Dr. Wilson shook his head. "Not just yet. It's too chaotic in there right now."

"Isn't there anything I can do? Besides just sit here?"

He reached for her hand and squeezed it. "You can pray." Then he disappeared into her mother's room.

Pray. Amy pondered his advice. She couldn't remember the last time she had prayed. She had been raised in a Christian home. Although she did not remember her father ever setting his foot inside a church, Granny Dix went all the time. She went several times during the week and twice on Sunday. Over the years she had sung in the choir and taught Sunday school. She had made tons of peanut brittle for church fund raisers and helped at summer camp. Young mothers were always seeking her counsel about homes and husbands and sick and ailing children. She had served God in many ways. Amy remembered her mother as always busy with the church, yet she never neglected her home. Amy didn't know how anyone could do it. With her own busy schedule now, she knew there would be no time for church, even if she wanted to go.

When she was smaller, Amy went along. She had enjoyed Sunday school, and even the worship services had been lively and interesting. But when she was older—maybe about Bethany's age now—she had become disillusioned with the other young people. They seemed to gossip a lot and hurt each other's feelings, and Amy got enough of that at school. She had needed acceptance and friendship when she went to church, not hurt and criticism. She knew in her heart that was no excuse, but she didn't have the strength to fight it.

Amy remembered one loud argument between her parents, and that was at the time she announced her intention to stop going to church. As usual, her father's deep voice was the loudest. "No, Dixie, I will not force her to go. She's old enough to make her own decisions about these things."

"Hogwash," Granny Dix replied. "She's just a child. We have every right to require that she attend church."

"I will not force religion down anyone's throat."

"Things would be a lot easier around here," his wife retorted, "if somebody would force it down *your* throat. Maybe I've made a mistake, keeping quiet all these years."

"Church is for sissies and old ladies," her father said. "You can go if you want to. I've never stood in your way, Dixie, and Amy can go—but only if she wants to."

A long silence followed, and Amy listened carefully. "Jack, you're making a mistake. Teenagers need God, maybe more than anyone else. Amy's headed for trouble, without the influence of the church."

But he was adamant, unbudging. Part of Amy had yearned for her parents to insist that she go. Deep down, she knew she needed the church. She was smart enough to realize it had played an important part in protecting her from activities that really would have been harmful. And she wanted the firmness of both parents' convictions. She wanted to be guided and instructed. Amy had enough burdens, enough decisions that only she could make. It would be such a relief if her parents would help out by taking some of the load.

But then there was that other part of Amy, too, that was in rebellion. Don't tell *me* what to do, it said. She was old enough, thank you, to decide these things for herself. That part of Amy was delighted that she would not have to go back to church. But that part of Amy also felt empty. She eventually tried to fill the void with all kinds of worldly things, but nothing had ever succeeded in filling the emptiness.

And as for prayer. Amy knew her mother had never ceased to pray, but now Granny Dix needed someone to pray for her, the way she had always prayed for everyone else. And Amy was out of practice. She wouldn't even know where to begin. But if she had known the battle that lay ahead of her, she would have dropped to her knees right then and there and started to call on the name of the Lord.

* * * * *

It was several hours before Amy heard from Cliff. She had left messages all around town, and it irritated her that she couldn't talk to him when she needed him. She was still sitting outside Dixie's room when a nurse informed her that she had a phone call at the nurses' station. Amy lifted the receiver to hear Cliff. "How's your mom?"

"Still unconscious."

"Stroke?"

"It looks like it. They're working on her now, still doing some tests. Can you come, Cliff? I need you."

"I would like to, honey," Cliff said, "but that's why I was calling. I'm on my way out of town."

"To where?"

"I've got to zip over to New Orleans. The Mothers' Ark project has some kinks in it that have to be ironed out."

Amy bristled. Lorene Fields again, her thorn in the side. "How long do you plan to be gone?"

"A few days."

"Cliff, I do need you. I wouldn't ask if it wasn't important."

A long silence. "Man, I'm sorry, honey. But you're tough. You'll be all right."

A dead feeling crept into Amy's heart, and she bit back her tears. Oh, Cliff! she cried inside. She spoke, "Yeah, I'll be all right. Go ahead, Cliff. Have fun."

"I'm not going there to have fun, I—"

"You devil!"

"Amy, listen—"

But the phone was dead. Amy had already hung up.

10

Living Will

Hours stretched into days, and still Amy waited for her mother to sit up and talk and act normal again. But the older woman just lay there in her bed, silent and still, an i.v. line running into her left arm. She was able to breathe with the respirator, and Amy sat quietly looking at her mother, hoping that any minute now she would open her eyes. "Mother?" Amy waited in the silence, which was broken only by the dreadful hiss of the respirator. Amy hated that noise. It reminded her of a movie she had seen once in which someone had died while connected to a large, square machine just like this one beside her mother's bed. Hiss, hiss, it sounded into the chilled quietness. Amy shivered, and a giant wave of nausea swept over her.

"Mother, can you hear me?" Amy waited expectantly for some sign of recognition. The dear old face was gray, the folds of skin hanging. Amy traced the lines with her eyes, remembering days when the skin was smooth and pink. Dixie had been in her thirties when Amy was born, so Amy's memories were not of what might be called youth, but her memories were of young days filled with vitality and energy and good health. Suddenly Amy longed for those days! She longed to be a little girl again, sheltered by her mother's strength, finding refuge in her fragrant comfort when the world was rough and hard.

What wondrous times there were, coming home from school to a neat and tidy house filled with pine-scented aromas, mingled with the unmistakable, sweet smell of brownies just about ready to come out of the oven. And being met in the kitchen by the short little lady called Mama. Amy would bury her face in the crisp, clean apron as she embraced her mother, and all the little hurts of the day would melt into nothingness. Through the years, in times of weakness she could always count on Mama's strength. Now the tables were turned, and she would have to be the source of strength for her mother. But how could she? Amy felt she would crumble any minute now.

She had never given much thought to death until her father passed away two years ago. But death was a hard thing. Amy choked back a sob. She did not want to think about her mother dying! Surely she would get well any day now and come back home, and they would all hear her funny stories again. Oh, Mother!

Suddenly Amy became aware of someone beside her and looked up to see Cliff. Bitter memories of their last coversation forgotten, Amy slid into his arms. For a long moment, her husband held her close, stroking her hair and cooing words of sweet comfort. Amy gathered strength from his arms and from the familiar, manly scent of his cologne. The stiff, starched collar brushed against her cheek, and her fingers stroked the expensive texture of his suit.

"How is she, honey?"

"Oh, Cliff, she just lies there."

Cliff pulled one of the little chairs away from the wall and sat beside his wife, peering at the unconscious form on the bed. "What does the doctor say?"

"They don't really know what's going on with Mama. She had another stroke last night in her sleep."

"How are the girls holding up?"

"Fine. Jennifer's been up here a lot, keeping her eye on her grandma. She had to go to Sacramento. Something to do with the house."

"The house should be just about ready, shouldn't it?"

Amy nodded. The kids had bought a really old and dilapidated house and were in the process of renovating it. "In fact," said Amy, "it's far enough along that they can live in it right now."

Cliff sighed. "I guess we're really losing our little girl."

"They would have left already, but for Mother. They'll have to make the move soon, though, because of campaign strategy."

Cliff leaned back and studied his wife. "Why are you rooting for Rich Meyers? Isn't he one of those prolife candidates?"

Amy blinked. "I don't know. I never thought about it one way or the other. He's just an honest man, and goodness knows, we need that."

Cliff sighed. "Well, what do you plan to do about your mother?"

"I don't know. They say all they can do is help her rest comfortably."

"Is she going to wake up again, or what?"

"Cliff, I told you, they don't know yet."

Cliff looked at his mother-in-law for a long moment. "Is she in pain, do you know?"

Amy shook her head. "They say she's not. One thing, though. They're concerned about pneumonia. Her lungs are still very weak from the fire." Amy's eyes began to fill with tears. She sat ummoving, her head resting in her hand, stiff and tense.

"Amy," asked Cliff, "are you all right?"

"She's not going to make it, Cliff. My mama's not going to make it!"

* * * * *

Amy was standing at the window in the waiting room when the sun came up. This had always been her favorite time of day. The death of the darkness, the birth of a brand-new beginning. Amy had spent many dawns enraptured with the colorful drama unfolding before her like a giant canvas. But this was different.

An awful gnawing in the pit of her stomach told Amy things would never be the same again. A dismal trumpet had sounded, ending some part of her life that she was not even able to define.

She had just left her mother's room, and a part of her had remained behind. What she had seen in that room had left her reeling with horror. It seemed that every monstrous tube and machine imaginable was attached to the dear, still form, only to keep the very basic functions going. Amy startled herself by digging her teeth into the back of her hand. She had been lost in her world of thought. "Oh, Mama," she cried, "oh, Mama . . ."

Cliff and Dr. Wilson came into the empty lounge, Cliff bringing his wife a cup of steaming coffee fresh from the nurses' station. He watched in amazement as she gulped down the full cup of hot liquid, unmindful of its intense temperature. "Dr. Wilson, what's going to happen to my mama?"

The kind, old doctor looked straight into her eyes. "I honestly don't know at this point, Amy. I wish I could give you some hope."

"Do you mean she's . . . terminal?"

"If by terminal you mean that her death is imminent, no. Although it is not likely, she could recover at any time and live a normal life. Most probably, she will remain as she is indefinitely and will eventually die."

"You mean, she will probably just lie there like that for months or even years? Hooked up to those awful machines?" Dr. Wilson nodded. "Do you know if she—if she—I mean, have you done any tests on her brain?"

"Of course. So far the EEG shows enough activity to rule out any real damage in that area."

"What're all those machines for?"

"Those are what's keeping your mother alive right now."

"Those terrible things?"

Dr. Wilson nodded. "Those and God."

"One thing," said Amy. "Mother always insisted she did not want any extraordinary efforts to keep her alive. Daddy didn't have all those machines, and Mama didn't want them either."

"That is a serious decision, Amy," cautioned Cliff.

Dr. Wilson said, "Your mother does have a living will, Amy. That pretty much spells out her wishes. Were you aware of it?"

"No, what's a living will?"

"It's a special document that is becoming more and more popular, especially among the elderly. The basic idea is okay, in that patients do need some control over their treatment, but there is some potential for confusion or abuse, especially if it is not worded properly. Anyway, she put one together shortly after your father died, because they had such a hard time getting him off all the equipment."

"Getting him off?"

"The hospital felt they should do everything to prolong his life, even when it was evident his hours were few. That wasn't what he wanted, but it was hard to convince the hospital. All he wanted was to die comfortably, in God's own time. He wanted his food and water, but nothing else."

Amy's eyes smarted. She asked, "What does this living will say?"

"It's standard wording about her being allowed to die naturally and not be kept alive by artificial means and heroic measures."

She nodded. "Mother once told me that when God's ready, He'll take her to heaven. She didn't want us holding her back when that time came. This looks like it could be that time, doesn't it?"

Cliff took Amy by her elbow and led her to a little,

vinyl, love seat. "Do you realize what you're saying, honey?"

"I'm saying Mama would not want to exist indefinitely with all those monstrosities all over her. What would happen, Doctor, if you took them all away?"

The older man shrugged his shoulders as though there were a heavy burden on them. "It's possible that she would continue breathing on her own, but in all probability, she would die."

"But only if that's God's choice. I know my mom. I know how much she trusts her Lord." Amy, numb but aware of the weighty decision in her words, said, "Take them away."

"You're absolutely certain?"

Amy nodded and turned to face the wall. "Okay, Lord, it's all in Your hands now."

11

Mothers' Ark Comes to Town

The big house sat on a knoll, its pale-blue paint glistening in the sun. It was a two-storied delight, and Amy Harper almost expected to see Scarlett O'Hara in all her southern finery step out onto the veranda. It was a sweltering late summer afternoon, muggy, and with not a trace of a breeze. She wiped the perspiration off her forehead with one of the lacy handkerchiefs Granny Dix had given her last Christmas and then turned her attention to what the mayor was saying.

"We are so honored to gather here this afternoon," his voice boomed over the loudspeaker, "to participate in the opening of this worthy new facility."

Amy tried to listen attentively, because what he was saying now contradicted something he had said at a recent meeting of the city council. There he had talked about how welfare mothers should abort their babies to save taxpayers money. Now he was extolling the virtue of welfare mothers bearing and raising their offspring.

Amy stood at the edge of the crowd, thinking about how she had usually been on the edge of every gathering she had ever attended. Never really belonging anywhere, she always stood on the outside looking in. Now her dark eyes swept over the crowd and rested on Cliff. He had not seen Amy arrive and was standing beside Lorene Fields. Next to her was the president of her board of directors, also from New Orleans. Amy studied them carefully. She watched as Cliff and Lorene would turn and look at one another and nod their heads in agreement over something that was being said. They obviously agreed on many things. Amy, deeply tanned in her white linen suit, could have passed for Lorene's sister.

As she continued to watch Cliff and Lorene, she saw their hands touch lightly at one point. Just a touch that a casual observer might have taken as accidental. But having been on the receiving end of Cliff's touch for so many years, Amy recognized the meaning, the tender feeling, that lay behind it. And somewhere, deep inside of her, something died in that moment with that touch.

When the mayor's message ended, the tour of the house began. Amy moved along with the crowd. It was a lovely facility, and four women were scheduled to move in this week. The first one would be along this afternoon, as a matter of fact. At this rate, it would be filled to capacity in no time. All the women scheduled to arrive so far were from other states. A while back the Supreme Court had given the individual states the authority to make their own decisions about the abortion issue, and several states, as a result, had clamped down tightly with new and restrictive laws. Facilities like Mothers' Ark were springing up all over the country to house the women who were now having their babies instead of abortions. But California seemed to go in the opposite direction after these new decisions. Amy remembered Rich Meyers talking about it in a campaign speech, calling the state a veritable death chamber. She smiled wryly and thought that was a good way to lose an election.

On the ground floor was a kitchen and a large, homey dining room. The girls themselves would prepare their meals, each taking turns with different aspects of the preparation. A spacious living room was just off the entry hall, decorated in colors of muted greens and blues. The contrast was refreshing. Other recreational areas were downstairs, including a game room, classrooms, and even an exercise room. The sleeping rooms were upstairs, five in all. Colorful rugs sprawled on the glistening hardwood floors, matching thick, fluffy comforters. Tall, wide windows graced each room, with a view that extended for seemingly unending miles across the green and fertile valley.

Amy was impressed. It was all so lovely, so comfortable, so cozy and homey. If she were an unmarried mother-to-be, she would not mind staying here, not one bit.

"Amy!" Startled, she looked toward the sound. Cliff, still beside Lorene Fields, was beckoning her, and Amy joined them. "Amy, I'm glad you made it," Cliff was saying, a large smile across his face. "Come meet Lorene Fields. Lorene, Amy, my wife."

Up close, Lorene looked even taller, almost larger than life. The word that kept spinning through Amy's mind was "voluptuous." Next to Lorene, Amy felt small, insignificant, acutely aware of her own slender frame. Her tiny hand became lost in Lorene's hearty, robust one, and Amy felt she was being consumed by the larger woman's shadow. She could think of only one thing at this point, and that was to run back to the safety of her own private office at the magazine. Amy did not belong here; she felt like an intruder.

"I'm so glad you could come, Amy. I've read some of your articles."

Amy blinked. "All the way back in New Orleans?"

"Our worlds are much closer than you realize."

Amy was not certain what that meant. She just stared at the woman for a moment and then asked, "I assume from the nature of this project that you're one of those prolifers?"

Lorene smiled. "I'm on your side, Amy," she said. "But I'm on their side, too."

Amy was confused, and although she could not explain it, she suddenly felt very soiled. "I don't see how you can sit on the fence like that."

"In other words," Lorene went on, "I'm on the *woman's* side."

Cliff cleared his throat. "I think what Lorene means is that, while she doesn't believe in abortion for herself, personally, she would not deny anyone else the right to have one. Is that right, Lorene?"

"Cliff," she said cooly, "while that may be a part of what I mean, I am perfectly capable of speaking for myself."

The two women exchanged a sudden look of understanding. In spite of herself, Amy felt a flicker of sympathy for Lorene.

Cliff pressed right on. "Amy is for abortion. I am against it."

Amy's head jerked toward her husband. "Are you? I didn't know that. I'd always assumed—"

"Oh, don't worry, Amy; I'm not the enemy. I certainly don't consider myself prolife." Both women were staring at him curiously. He shifted weight, standing awkwardly for a moment, and then went on. "What I mean is, I am against abortion, not because I'm into the idea of life, but because of what abortion does to women psychologically. It destroys them emotionally."

Satisfied with his own answer, Cliff turned and led the way through the rest of the tour, Lorene at his side.

After all the proper words and gestures, Amy finally made her escape, declining the offer to partake of refreshments from the long oak table in the dining room. It was not until she had reached the safety and sanctity of her own office that she collapsed. Pictures of Cliff and Lorene tumbled at her from the deep, hurt-filled caverns of her mind. How on earth, she cried out, does a wife accept something as devastating as this? Her readers and her writers alike would all agree that the wife should throw the man away. But deep down, where she felt the heartbreak, Amy knew she would never do that. She knew that she would cling to her husband and to her marriage with all her might. She could never let him go. What frightened her the most was the gnawing thought that it was Cliff himself who wanted to be free. She laid her head on her French provincial desk and wept.

* * * * *

She must have dozed off there at her desk, because the buzzing of her intercom startled her. Her head hurt. "Yes, Barbara?"

Her secretary's voice informed her that Jay Gilt was on the line; would she like to talk with him? Amy groaned. He was putting on the pressure about that article, and she knew there was no way she could, in good conscience, print such a piece. Not without sacrificing the excellence she strove for and that she owed to her readers. "Yes, Jay, how are you?"

"Fine, thank you. How's the magazine business?"

"Great, just great," Amy replied. "Our advertisers and subscribers almost doubled last month alone."

"Good girl," he crooned. Amy winced. Good girl. When would this president of the board get the revelation that this was a feminist magazine and that he was dealing with real, flesh-and-blood feminists? "So. Which issue will my article be appearing in?"

"None of them."

"Why not?"

Amy was weary. "I already explained. This is a publication for upbeat feminists. I just don't see how your article ties in with that philosophy—at least not in its present form. Perhaps you could—"

"Women need to know they have the *right* to die, along with all their other rights."

"I understand what you're trying to say," Amy countered, "but really now, we have always had that right."

"I'm afraid I don't follow you."

"Everybody has the right to decline medical treatment. They always have had that right. So your article does not contribute anything to the issue of women's rights. What your article *does* do is promote the deliberate killing of people."

"Not killing them. Honoring their own wish to die painlessly when there is no hope of survival anyway."

Amy frowned. "But you're talking about active measures, such as injection by a doctor."

Jay cleared his throat impatiently.

"Perhaps," Amy suggested, "you'd like to do a story on housing, or employment practices? If so, I'd love to see it. We need more stuff in those areas."

"Amy, I am very tired of hounding you to do this article."

"Then stop." Amy felt fire course up and down her backbone. "Mr. Gilt, I have tried very hard to be kind and not hurt your feelings. But I feel you have pushed me into speaking just what is on my mind. Number one, your article is depressing. You include no positive elements in it, none at all. All you talk about is causing people to die. Number two, our readership requires a positive, uplifting approach, with a strong take-away value. If you rewrote your piece—"

"Is this your final word, or will you reconsider?"

Amy sighed. "Mr. Gilt, when the board appointed me as editor of this magazine, it also bestowed on me the power to do my job. Part of that job is to review manuscripts and decide whether or not they are suitable for the publication. I have fulfilled those duties with your submission, so there is nothing to reconsider. I will return your manuscript to you in the evening's mail—unless, of course, you'd rather drop by and pick it up."

"Good day, Mrs. Harper. You'll be hearing from me."

Amy placed the phone back into its cradle. "Come on in," she called out to the person she knew was lurking behind the closed office door. The door opened at once and Barbara bounced in.

"Amy, you're in for it!"

"But why?" Amy was having great difficulty understanding what the hullabaloo was all about. To her, it was simple.

"Jay Gilt has a lot of clout."

"Why?"

Barbara shrugged. "Probably because of his family fortune. Did you know his father and two brothers own *The Post?*"

Amy sat up straight. "What? He's *that* Gilt?"

Barbara was slowly nodding her head. Now, too late, Amy had begun to understand.

12

Fired!

A special meeting of the board of directors was called for the next morning. Amy made her way down the hall to the conference room, where all the board meetings were held. When she took her place at the conference table, there were already five people present, three men and two women. One of the women, obviously the secretary, was looking around and recording the names of those present. The other woman, Carla Coleman, busied herself looking through her personal organizer, flipping pages, making notes here and there. Jay Gilt, of course, was presiding.

"Meeting called to order," he began, sparing all preliminaries. "This is a special meeting of the executive committee of the board of directors of the She Corporation, called at the request of the president. Its purpose," he went on, pacing himself to be sure that the secretary took down all he was saying, "is to discuss the competence of the editor of *She* magazine and to evaluate her performance."

Amy's eyebrows shot up. Discuss her competence?

Jay Gilt went on to explain the situation to the committee, that the editor had refused to print a relevant article, and that she had, in doing so, displayed intractable qualities. To be editor of such a magazine as *She,* he went on, one must be flexible, giving, able to flow with the trends. Jay Gilt explained patiently that it was the lack of those qualities in Amy, more than just a mere article, that caused his concern. In essence, he was stressing, to be so intractable this early in the game, what would she be like later on? Since Amy was still serving her probationary period, now was the time to take up this matter.

After a short discussion among the members, Jay Gilt turned again to Amy. "Mrs. Harper, we appreciate the quality of your work and recognize that, in terms of time, you have gone over and above duty. We would really like to retain you on staff as our editor. The truth is, we'd really hate to lose you. You're a good, qualified worker. It is not our desire, nor the purpose of this meeting, to fire you. We want to come to an understanding that we can all live with."

Amy's head was swimming. Fire her? Suddenly she realized how utterly unprepared she was for this meeting. The sad fact was, there was really no way she could have prepared.

"What we have to determine today is whether or not your goals and philosophies are the same as the goals and philosophies of the magazine you are representing." All the members nodded in agreement. "If they are, then we have no problem. If they are not the same, then it's best to know that now, so that we can all cut our losses short."

Well, Amy thought, he was making himself clear; he was having no problem in communicating today. For the first time Carla Coleman closed her organizer and leaned forward. "Amy," she said, her gray eyes looking straight at Amy, "what I'd like to know is, did you refuse to print Jay's article, and if so, why?"

Amy cleared her throat. "I did refuse to print it, at least in its present form." So far, so good. "As to why, it was because I did not see any relevance to the issues my magazine deals with."

"Thank you. I understand," Carla said softly. "It would appear to me, however, that the right to die *is* a legitimate women's concern. Isn't it?"

"So is the other side of the coin, the right to live."

Jay Gilt interrupted. "Mrs. Harper, there's no need to repeat yourself again. It has become obvious to me just what the problem is. It's the situation you're going through with your mother. It has, perhaps, clouded your judgment?"

"Why do you bring that up? You and I had our disagreement before this ever happened to my mother."

But Jay Gilt rushed on. "You had support systems removed from her, didn't you?"

"Yes," Amy admitted. "And you see there are no guarantees, because she is still alive in spite of it."

Jay's eyes penetrated hers. "You took her off all artificial treatments?"

"Yes."

"All of her tubes, then, are removed?"

"Yes, except for feeding, of course."

"Why haven't you had that removed?"

Amy blinked. "Her food and water?"

Jay Gilt nodded. "Artificial treatment keeps her alive against nature's wishes, don't you think?"

Amy, dismayed, responded sharply. "I cannot understand your reasoning. All life—plants, animals, everything —requires food and water. They're absolutely necessary to everybody, sick or healthy." Gilt looked at her blankly. "My mother does not have some terminal illness, Mr. Gilt. She could wake up tomorrow and be fine again. I cannot withhold her food and water; that would mean causing her death."

Jay Gilt leaned back in his chair and made a show of crossing his long, burly arms. He was obviously making some kind of nonverbal statement. His eyes moved around the table, looking at each of the committee members. Then he spoke: "Amy, I don't mean to sound unkind, but it would appear that you've let your emotions for your mother cloud your sound editorial judgment in this case. Am I right?"

"Am I on trial here, or what?" It was Amy's turn to move her eyes around the table. All the faces seemed to reflect that their owners were following their president's lead. Amy did not want to lose this job. She loved the work; it had been rich and fulfilling and had added a new dimension to her life. The magazine had even become a better one under her leadership—not folded, as she had feared. Readership had jumped thirty-one percent.

Her new fear now was that, if she spoke the truth, she would have to give all this up. She and the board had reached an impasse; either they would give, or she must.

And it was obvious, from the oppressive silence that hung in the room, that they were not about to budge.

It would be easy right now to lay the blame at her mother's feet. Jay had given her that alternative, and it was one that others would be able to understand and work around. If she chose that route, the board would be willing to be lenient and work with her until she had settled the emotional issue in her own mind. And then she could keep her job and continue to accomplish good things for women. Surely the ends would justify the means. But that would not be honest.

Finally, she spoke: "In a way, you are right, Mr. Gilt. My mother's experience has opened my eyes about a lot of things. It has given me a new perspective about life and how fragile it is, how truly precious. But I can't say that it has 'clouded' my thinking. This issue between you and me came up before my mother's experience. I fail to see how your article on death relates to the goals of *She* magazine, and I am hard pressed to see how this issue alone can result in my termination. It's a silly issue."

"It's a vital issue."

"Not if you leave me alone to run the magazine as I see fit. You hired me to put out a quality magazine every month. I've done that, plus a whole lot more."

Folders began closing around the table. The secretary shut her minutes book. "Well, Mrs. Harper," asked Jay Gilt, "we would like to have your answer."

"You really don't leave me much choice." Amy swallowed hard. "I have to stand by my original decision."

"Then you don't really leave us much choice, either, Mrs. Harper. Good day. We'll be in touch."

13

Bethany's Revelation

When Amy cleaned out her desk at the office, Barbara stood by wordlessly. She had gone through this with other bosses. Amy went through the motions like an automaton, quietly, steadily, without emotion. Once Barbara lamented, "I'm so sorry, Amy. I'll really miss you."

"I've enjoyed you, too, Barbara."

"Have you thought about suing?"

"Suing? No."

"Sounds to me like you have a good case."

"I doubt it. I was still on probation, which means they really don't even have to have a reason to terminate me. Besides . . ."

"Besides, what?"

"I don't want to work for a board like that. I have to be me. I have to do what I think is right. I can't be kowtowing to them all the time. What would it be next time? It's just not worth it to me; life's too short."

"If you win, though, you would probably be able to

set your own rules."

"I truly, truly doubt it. Anyway, we have to set our priorities, and burning out all my energies in litigation is not high on my list."

As Amy drove home that day, she thought all the bad that could happen had already happened. Her marriage had seemingly reached the point of being beyond repair. Her little Cessna lay wrecked at the airport, and a mechanics' strike was raging. Worse than that, though, was the fear Amy felt in her heart. She secretly hoped they'd never get around to repairing her plane; that way, she would not have to fly again. The cowardice tore at her self-esteem, bringing on bouts of depression.

And then her mother was comatose in the hospital and might never recover. She had recently developed some sort of an infection and was on a program of antibiotics. The stress was incredible. And Amy was surprised by how deeply she missed Jennifer since her daughter had moved to the capital. Amy felt such a loss, even though they kept in close touch. And now—now, on top of it all—she had lost her job, and her career was shipwrecked. Oh, Jennifer, she thought, come home. I need you!

Amy felt all life had been drained out of her as she crawled home that afternoon. Tired and weary, she looked forward to a hot bath, plenty of solitude, and a good book. As she made her way down the hallway to her bedroom, Bethany's bathroom door was ajar, and Bethany was retching noisily. Amy flew across Bethany's room and found her daughter sitting on the floor beside the toilet. "Bethany, you're sick!"

The girl continued to vomit for a few minutes, with Amy wiping her forehead with a wet washcloth. A final swipe across her lips, and Bethany rested her head on Amy's breast. "Oh, Mama, Mama."

"Yes, dear?"

"Amy, I'm home!"

"That's your dad, sweetheart." Amy wondered why she was whispering.

"Oh, Mama, don't let him get me!"

"Get you?" Amy held her daughter away from her, looking at her quizzically. "Why would your father want to get you?"

Bethany responded by collapsing into loud sobs. Cliff appeared at the door, and Amy motioned for him to wait outside, all dreams of restful solitude forgotten.

When the two women joined Cliff, Bethany flew across the kitchen and dove into his arms. He held the girl, letting her cry. Finally the sobs began to subside and Bethany began to talk, swallowing huge gulps of air in between her words. "Oh, Daddy, I'm so sorry!"

"Sorry? Sorry for what, babe?"

"Oh, Daddy . . ." Cliff shot a helpless, frustrated look at his wife. Amy remained silent. "Daddy, I'm going to have a baby."

Cliff blinked. Amy remained unmoving, still. "Baby?" His fingers momentarily loosed his hold on his daughter, and she clung even tighter. "Baby?" he repeated numbly. "What are you talking about?"

"Daddy, please—!"

"I cannot believe this," wailed Amy. "I don't believe this is happening; it's some kind of nightmare."

"Mom, I'm sorry. I didn't mean for it to happen."

Cliff was patting her shoulder absently, forcing himself to be steady. "There, there, it's okay." Holding his daughter away from him, his hands on her plump young shoulders, he looked into those blue eyes so much like his own. Then he led her gently down the step and into the family room. Amy followed in silence. "Bethany," Cliff said as they took their seats, "why didn't you come to me with this problem? Didn't you trust me?"

"Cliff, please," interrupted Amy. "That won't solve anything."

Bethany dropped her eyes, staring at her fingernails. Cliff noticed that the nails which had been long just a few weeks ago were now short and nubby.

Amy asked, "Cliff, what do you want to do?"

"What are our options?"

"Of course abortion is a very real option. But I—"

"Stop it!" shouted Bethany. "See what you two are doing? You're talking about me as though I'm not even here!"

Cliff was annoyed. "Bethany," he said with forced patience, "please let your mother and me talk." When she settled back down into the rich leather couch, he asked, "How far along are you?"

"Four months."

"Four months!" Cliff was shocked. His eyes shot to her midriff, which did not look pregnant at all to him, much less four months. "Are you sure?"

"I know when it happened. There was only one time. It happened when—"

Cliff interrupted his daughter. "I don't want to hear

the details," he said. "Have you seen a doctor?"

Bethany nodded her head. "And he verified all this?" Again she nodded. "Well," Cliff went on, "abortion is not even an option at this point anyway."

"Why not?"

"At four months?"

Bethany stared at her father with huge, round eyes. "Daddy, where have you been? Abortion is legal all the way up to the time of delivery!"

Cliff was shocked. "Who told you that?"

"The health clinic at school. They know all about these things."

All of this was proving to be just too much for Cliff. He looked beseechingly at Amy. "She's right, dear. Abortion's legal the entire nine months. But don't feel bad—most people aren't aware of it."

"How can that be?" He spoke the question aloud, more to himself than anyone else. No one bothered to answer him. "This clinic at school . . . is that where you kids get your birth control pills?" Bethany nodded, tears still filling her eyes. "A lot of good they did you, eh?"

"They gave me some," she said, "but I never took them."

"Why not?"

"Because I didn't plan on anything happening."

"Dumb kids."

"Daddy, I don't know of anybody who bothers taking those things."

"Well," Cliff finally said, his eyes meeting Bethany's, "what do you want to do?"

"I want an abortion."

Cliff looked at her thoughtfully. Then he looked at Amy. "I don't think so," he said at last. "I don't think that's the answer."

"But I have a right to an abortion."

"Bethany, hush."

She started crying again. "See? I knew you'd refuse. That's why I didn't want you to know anything about it!"

"Listen," demanded Cliff, "how did you think you could pull something like this off without your mother and me knowing about it?" He stared at his daughter as if he were seeing her for the first time. She looked hard, stubborn, cold. When had she grown to look like that? What had happened to the soft and tender little girl Cliff had known just a short time ago?

Her eyes, dry now, met his fully. "Daddy, the kids do it all the time. There's no law that says we have to have your permission."

"In this house, there is. Now leave your mother and me alone."

"Daddy, please."

"Go to your room." Bethany continued to sit there, stiff, her jaw set. "Now." She jerked herself up from the couch and out of the room, howling all the way to her room.

Cliff turned to Amy. "You knew about this all along?"

"Of course not."

"Would you have let her have an abortion? Behind my back?"

Amy was so tired that she wished she could just get away from all this. "I haven't had time to think about it one way or the other, Cliff."

"I've heard you say so many times that abortion is a woman's right. That it's her body."

Amy stared numbly at the brass urn by the door. She felt silly. She had said that. Abortion was one of the issues feminists had taken an official stand on. The rights of women were all wrapped up in the issue of abortion. But somehow this was different. This was her daughter's body . . . or is a baby actually a part of anybody else's body? Prolifers maintained that the baby's body was individual, separate from its mother's body. Could that be correct? "Cliff, just because I work for abortion rights does not mean I go around signing everybody up to have them."

"Well, then you do agree with me? About not letting her have one?"

"She's a fourteen-year-old child. What on earth is she going to do with a baby?"

"I don't know."

"Well, we have to think about those things. And you. Are you ready to be a grandfather? Because you'll be stuck with a lot of babysitting. Face it, our Bethany has a lot of growing up to do."

"Oh, Amy." Cliff stood up and walked to the window. Pulling the heavy gold draperies back, he peered outside. It was a lovely sunny afternoon, a good day to be outside doing fun things. This was not the time to be inside, stuck in gloom and mire and oppression. Cliff just stood there for a few long moments staring out the window, looking over the vast acreage of land that he could call his own. Then he turned and looked at his wife. "Amy, I'm almost fifty. I'll be honest with you; I feel old enough as it is, without being a grandfather. No, I really am not ready for that. I want to live first, have fun, kick up my heels."

Amy just looked at him. Grateful that he was opening up his feelings to her, she did not answer. She just gave him the silence, the freedom, to talk. He went on, "All my life I've been loaded down with responsibility. First, having to quit school so young. And having all the care of my mother and brothers and sisters on my shoulders. Then I put them all through school, then myself. Then I had my own family to bring up. Jennifer's grown, married now. And Bethany—she's still got years of high school left." He turned back to the window, looking out again. "I'm not complaining. Really, I don't regret a minute I've given to you and the girls. I'd do it all again. But I'm tired, Amy."

Amy felt a sudden chilling apprehension. "What are you saying?"

He walked over and sat down on the couch, leaning his upper body forward to rest on his knees. "What am I saying? I don't know. I honestly don't know."

Amy was holding her breath in sheer terror. Somehow, she sensed what was coming. And she knew she could not handle it. Not now. Not yet. In spite of all her efforts to be a feminist—independent, strong—she was not ready for what she knew Cliff was going to end up doing. Her head was spinning and she had a thousand questions. The only thing, she couldn't think of what they were right now. She had heard other women talk, feminists. They said that a women can be better off without a man to hold her down, pin her to the ground, and destroy her dreams. They felt a woman could perhaps accomplish more when she had only her own goals, her own programs, to focus her energies on.

But these were stronger women, maybe, and Amy felt so weak, so vulnerable. Maybe her friends were strong enough to make it alone. But Amy loved Cliff. She needed Cliff. Since she was fifteen years old, it had only been Cliff. Cliff was all she knew.

"Well," Cliff went on, changing gears, "what about Bethany?"

"I don't understand you, Cliff. You say she can't have the abortion, but you also say you don't want your grandchild."

Cliff gave a little chuckle. "Sounds mixed up, huh? But, Amy, there has to be a better way. I've seen what it's done to you. We can't put Bethany through all that. Please. Let's figure out some other solution for our child."

Amy sucked in her breath. "What are you talking about, 'done to me?' "

"Don't you think I know? I haven't loved you and cared for you all these years without getting to know you. Amy, I've watched the process you went through. I see what happened to you. It's almost destroyed you, Amy. You're only a shadow of the person you used to be and could have been."

Amy thought she would scream. She would rather deal with his leaving than deal with this. "Cliff, I don't want to talk about it."

"Maybe it's time you did. I've always regretted what we did, Amy. Haven't you ever regretted it?"

"I don't know what you're talking about," she said, standing up, "and I refuse to sit here and listen to this drivel."

"Amy, face it. We killed our baby."

"No!"

"Amy, we did. Thirty years ago, we did."

Her eyes flashed. "*You* did it, I didn't!"

"Amy—"

"Shut up, Cliff Harper, shut up. I won't listen to this. Just shut up!"

He stood up and faced her squarely. They looked at each other silently for a very long moment; then he turned and left the room. Amy knew it was only a matter of time before Cliff would leave her and end their marriage. And when that day came, she thought, she would not be ready. With a sinking feeling, Amy realized that her very survival depended on Cliff Harper. And she hated herself for her weakness.

14

Amy Gives Up

The day came, even sooner than she had expected. Finally she was face to face with the knowledge that he was walking out of her life. He had finally taken the plunge. His bags had been packed and moved into his new studio apartment downtown at the Towers.

Now he just stood there by the door, his hand poised on the knob, looking as though he were suspended between two realities. "I'm sorry, Amy. Really I am. Maybe after a separation for a while, maybe things will look different. Maybe then we can try again. But for now—"

"I know," she interrupted, her face screwed into a mimicking scowl. "You're tired. You need a rest. From your responsibilities. That's a bunch of hogwash."

"I'd like for you to see a counselor. Would you?"

Amy felt herself begin to grow furious in spite of her anguish. "Counselor! What would I see a counselor for? You talk like this whole thing is my fault. Why don't *you* see a counselor?"

Cliff let out a huge, patronizing sigh. He stood there calmly, analyzing her with those cool, blue eyes. That always made Amy even angrier. "You've been through a lot, emotionally, these past few months."

Oh, how she wanted to kill him! Instead, she spoke evenly through clenched teeth. "You just go on back—to *her*—and stay there."

"I'm not going to anybody."

Oh God, her heart screamed, *please don't leave me!* Her voice said: "I never want to see you again!"

"Honey, please—"

"I know you love her." Cliff's eyes fell, unable to meet hers any longer. Amy, noticing this, rushed on, "Don't you?"

"Amy, don't do this to yourself."

"Well? Answer me! Don't you? Don't you?"

"I suppose."

Amy's head was starting that awful spinning again; the nausea was rising in her throat. "Get out of here! Don't torture me like this."

He looked at her oddly. He measured his next words carefully. "I have the strangest feeling," he said, "that if I walk out of here now I'll never see you alive again."

His words pierced her spirit and sent chills down her back. He knew her so well, her husband. His soul was indeed knit with hers. From the depths of her being, she longed to fling herself into his arms and experience once again their strength and their comfort. She longed to cling tightly to him and have him stroke her hair once more and whisper that everything would be all right. *Just one more time,* her heart begged, *Just one more time . . .*

The futility of it all dulled her senses. Mercifully, her emotions became numb as the finality set in. It was over. He really meant it. If she were to go on with this life, it would be alone. Without him.

Without him? No. Amy couldn't do that. She thought she had already felt all the pain that this world had to offer her, but nothing had really prepared her for this day. She had loved him for over thirty years. But the marriage was dead. Dead, but she had refused to bury it. Surely, by the sheer force of her love it could be revived, sustained!

Then, with one final gaze, he turned and disappeared through the door. Amy moved like a zombie to the window and watched as he got into his car, turned it around, and slowly drove away. Knowing she would never see him again unleashed a well of despair within her. Death loomed before her like a golden ring, and she began to hurry so she could soon be swallowed up in its seductive nothingness.

She padded down the carpeted hall, the long afghan swishing around her ankles. Her reflection in the mirror was one of a slim woman who was really quite lovely. Slender, with large, dark eyes that friends said made her look like a tragic Russian. She brushed her long, black hair until every strand was in place. She wanted to look nice when they found her. If Amy had ever been determined about anything, it was that she would never again see the sun come up.

She opened the fresh fifth of Scotch she had purchased for this occasion. Then she gathered all the bottles of pills she had been collecting from Granny Dix's private drugstore and sat down on the side of the huge bed. Granny Dix had all kinds of tranquilizers and sleeping pills in that little drugstore of hers, but none of them had ever been touched. Amy had dutifully seen that every prescription had been filled, over her mother's protests.

As she began the tedious procedure of swallowing the pills, the faces of her daughters swam before her eyes. She slammed the pill bottle onto the nightstand and began to race back and forth across the bedroom floor. Her steps melted into a slow, methodical pace, back and forth, back and forth.

Suddenly the phone shrilled into the stillness. Her breath caught, and she backed against the wall, staring at the phone. Amy dared not breathe. One ring, two. Insistently the awful sound swirled around her head, daring her to answer it. Her eyes, wild and glassy, were glued to the intrusive white instrument on the nightstand. All she had to do was pick it up, and she would be able to postpone her fate for a little while longer. Just a simple hello into the mouthpiece, and she would be in touch with life once more. Life. All she knew was death.

As suddenly as it began, the phone stopped. It had cut off in the middle of a ring with a great finality, and the room was again plunged into silence. All she could hear was the sound of the air conditioning vent whispering gentle, cold air into the room. The heavy curtains were drawn tightly shut, the sunshine peeking through the hairline crack. The spirit of death loomed large and cold throughout the house, stalking, prodding. Coaxing, calling. Seducing.

Amy stared at her reflection again in the mirror. Some feminist. All her big talk, her great plans. She was going to change the world with her little editorial job, and what happened? What a hypocrite. Mealy-mouth. Preaching one thing and doing another. Great big failure. All washed up. Amy wondered how many others were like that—was she the only pretender in the whole movement? Was she the only feminist who marched and preached one thing and secretly felt differently on the inside? Why couldn't one be a feminist, she lamented, and still be oneself?

As she sank onto the side of the bed again, the little faces floated before her eyes, and she longed to reach out and draw her children close. She could smell the soft, fresh scent of Bethany's hair as she bathed it with her tears. But this was the best thing for them. They had a worthless mother, a crazy mother. The girls would be better off with her out of the way. Remembering all the hopes and dreams she had spun around her family's future, Amy's heart broke just as surely as if someone used a hammer on it. The heaviness was beyond her endurance.

But there was that other little baby, too, her little son. He would be almost thirty years old now, had she let him live. Instead, he was in heaven somewhere, probably hoping she never made it there. But she wanted to see him! She wanted to hold him close to her breast and say, *I'm sorry. I'm so very sorry . . . forgive me!*

With a new determination, she began to gulp the pills as quickly as she could. Ten pills. Twenty, forty. Her living children were better off without her, and she needed to communicate with her dead son. Sugar-coated Mellaril and Thorazine. Big fat Quaaludes. They were the hardest to get down. The little Stellazines and Valiums she could gulp down a handful at a time. Amy's throat tightened in rebellion against the assault and tried to close up. Nausea swelled up from her stomach as the room began to spin. She must stay awake. She couldn't take the chance of falling asleep until she had taken enough pills to assure the end. Amy did not want to wake up to the horror of having her stomach pumped. No, now that she had decided on this course of action, she would see that it was done properly. One bottle, two . . . bottle after bottle emptied . . . until she could no longer swallow yet another pill. The nausea was awful. *Oh God, don't let me throw up!*

Amy took one final gulp of Scotch, and then she lay back on the bed and arranged the afghan around herself in neat, attractive folds. Somehow it was important that she look nice and not frighten anyone when they found her. "God," she whispered, "if You're there somewhere, please forgive me. Let my son forgive me." And with that, her eyes closed for what should be the very last time.

15

Secret Meeting

Cliff stepped off the elevator on the mezzanine and made his way into the Emerald Restaurant. The lunch crowd was beginning to arrive, and his eyes searched the place, looking for someone. Jay Gilt, at a table in the far corner, lifted a hand in greeting, waving Cliff over to his table.

After the preliminaries, they ordered lunch and sat back to wait. Cliff eyed his companion suspiciously. "Well, Gilt, why did you ask me to lunch?" His arms were folded across his chest, and he refused Gilt's offer of a cocktail.

"Mr. Harper, how is your mother-in-law?"

"She's hanging on."

Gilt made a clucking sound. "Too bad she has to suffer like that."

"They say she's not suffering."

"Do you believe that? Really?"

"What do you mean?"

Gilt shrugged his massive shoulders. "Put yourself in her place . . . lying there in the same position, day after day, unable to meet even your most basic needs. Worse still . . . where is her hope?"

Cliff felt a twinge of guilt, which he refused to entertain. "There really is no hope," he said.

"And you don't mind watching her suffer like that?"

"We've done all we can. She had never wanted any heroic-type efforts to keep her alive, so we had the machines all disconnected. But nothing happened. There's nothing else to do at this point but wait it out."

"Hmm. Must be terribly expensive."

Cliff shrugged.

"By the way," Gilt asked, "how is your wife? I heard she is in some sort of mental asylum?"

"Mental asylum?" Cliff echoed. *Is that what people are saying?* "She's getting some much-earned rest in the hospital, that's all."

"Oh? Which hospital?"

Cliff glared at him. "What's it to you?"

"Is she competent? Mentally, I mean."

Cliff noisily scraped his chair back and stood up. "That's none of your business. And wherever she is, you helped put her there."

"Mr. Harper—please sit down. Believe me, I have only your best interests at heart." After a long hesitation, Cliff took his seat. Jay Gilt resumed his conversation. "I don't know if you are aware that I serve on several boards in town. *She* magazine . . . Rogers Corporation . . .Death with Dignity . . ."

"Death with Dignity? What on earth is that?"

The waiter set salads on the table, refilled the water glasses, and hurried to his other tables. Jay Gilt, dipping some dressing onto his salad, said, "Medical technology has made tremendous advances in recent years. It is possible to sustain biological life far beyond the natural life span. The result is that a person lives so long past his natural capacity that life ceases to have any real meaning for the dying person. These people end up facing their last months knowing that there is really no future for them—no hope, as in your mother-in-law's case. They have only pain and indignities to look forward to, and they increasingly feel the pressure to hurry up and get out of the way. They realize they're running up vast medical bills, and that the treatment is, in essence, being wasted on them since there is no hope of recovery. "Most people feel they have a fundamental right to control their destinies by regulating their own medical care. One of these rights is to have their physician assist in hastening their death."

"How?"

Jay Gilt smiled. "I prepared an article recently which explained all this," he said, "but your wife refused to print it. Here—" Gilt reached into the briefcase that had been lying on an empty chair. "Take this along with you. It goes into detail."

Cliff's eyes scanned the neatly typed article. Jay Gilt sat quietly, picking the lettuce from between his teeth with his fingers.

Suddenly Cliff laughed. "I can't imagine any reputable doctor doing anything like this."

"You'd be surprised. A study was done recently, a

survey of six hundred physicians. Twenty-three percent said they had actually taken active steps—*active* steps, mind you—to bring about the death of one of their patients. They view helping a person who is suffering as a kind and compassionate act."

"What's so compassionate about giving someone a lethal injection? Isn't that killing?"

Gilt put his fork down and wiped his mouth with the heavy linen napkin. "Mr. Harper, it's not really *killing* anyone. It's ending the circumstances that are forcing a person to continue living in agony when it is their time to die."

"I remember Amy mentioning this article," said Cliff, drumming his fingers on the manuscript. "She believed that it is not right to help someone kill himself. And I must confess, I agree."

"In the usual sense, you're both right. But in the case of a terminally ill or comatose person, you're incorrect. Have you ever seen a person suffer for weeks with cancer and waste away? No one can look at someone like that and say it's better for them to live longer."

Cliff frowned, remembering Granny Dix. "But you're not talking about letting someone die naturally; you're talking about taking active measures to cause death. That's playing God. It sounds like something a veterinarian would do to an animal.

"Why should dogs and cats be treated with more compassion than human beings? A little shot, and the patient drifts off peacefully, painlessly. Anything else is cruel and callous and heartless. Absolutely."

The waiter finished serving their lunch. "Would there be anything else?"

Jay Gilt waved him off and turned back to his companion. "So anyway, take the article. Read it at your convenience. I just felt that, under the circumstances, you might be interested because of your mother-in-law's suffering. I had a feeling it would be taking its toll on you and your family."

"But what could we do in her case? I know her doctor would not agree to a lethal injection."

Gilt shrugged. "That's why we need to get legislation passed that will provide for lethal injections. But you could at least have him disconnect the tubes that supply food and water artificially."

"But how could we do that? She is in a coma, but she is not brain dead. I don't think Dr. Wilson would allow it."

"Mr. Harper. Doctors have been known to refuse to cooperate before. They have made noble, self-righteous attempts to interfere with the rights of a human being. And the courts have had to step in and set things straight."

"The courts?"

Gilt nodded emphatically. "That's becoming the only place these days where dispassionate decisions can be made. Many judges are finding that they have to order doctors, nurses, and hospitals to carry out these measures."

"You want me to believe that there are actually court orders for this kind of thing?"

"Yes. One hospital refused to cooperate, and the court ruled that the patient could be moved to a hospital willing to stop the feeding. Eight days later, the patient was mercifully released from his suffering. And there are many other cases. Read the article; it's well documented. You can check the cases out for yourself. I also talk about some other interesting law in there. As a lawyer yourself, you'll appreciate reading some of the court decisions. You'll see."

Jay Gilt picked up the tab, reached into his wallet, and withdrew cash. "I've got to be moving on," he said. "Think about what we've said here today. If you need any assistance—legal or otherwise, contact us." With that, he gathered up his briefcase and strode away from the table, leaving Cliff alone with his awesome thoughts.

* * * * *

After reading the article and thinking about Granny Dix's situation for a long time, Cliff finally left the Emerald Restaurant and drove by Dr. Wilson's office. The doctor was just returning from lunch, so he led Cliff into his private office immediately. Cliff thanked him, and explained the situation to him. He told the doctor he had just met with the leader of Death with Dignity and that he had informed him of some of the rights his mother-in-law had. He explained that he was very tired of seeing her suffer.

Dr. Wilson leaned back in his leather chair. "Are you asking me to kill Dixie?"

Cliff smarted. It sounded awful, when put that way. "Kill her? Of course not. I'm asking for doctor-assisted relief for her. She has suffered long enough."

"What, specifically, are you asking?"

"Couldn't you give her something to let her die peacefully?"

"Absolutely not!"

"Well, can you at least disconnect the artificial feeding tube?"

"I cannot do that either."

"What do you mean, you can't? My mother-in-law has rights."

"Yes, she does. As a legal matter, she has not authorized us to disconnect her feeding tubes. Most importantly, there is the moral consideration. She is not brain dead. She is not even brain damaged or terminally ill. We cannot deprive her of basic nutrition. She has the right to trust that we will provide her with food and water. She has the right to be kept as comfortable as possible. We're doing that. And she is not suffering."

Cliff eyed the doctor suspiciously. "What if she were suffering? What if she had a terminal illness?"

Dr. Wilson sighed. "Cliff, each case is different. A cancer death, for example, can be among the most painful there is. I recently had a patient with incurable cancer who decided to remain at home until she died instead of selecting intensive hospital care to prolong her last days. But Dixie doesn't have cancer. She is not expected to die as a matter of course. She could wake up at any moment and resume a normal life."

"But then again she probably won't."

The doctor shrugged again, pushed his chair back, and laboriously stood up. "She probably won't."

"And you refuse my request?"

Dr. Wilson nodded.

"Then I shall get a court to order that you do it."

Dr. Wilson looked at Cliff for a long time, his wise old eyes sad. "Cliff, I'm very sorry that you even approached me on this issue. I know Dixie's feelings on the matter. She would want her food and water. Amy would, too. Now, if there's nothing else, I must ask you to leave."

"Very well," Cliff said tersely. "I shall see you in court."

16

Goodbye, Granny Dix

Amy had slept well last night, in spite of the ruckus down the hall. Mandy Ellers had tried slashing her wrists again, and they had to put her in seclusion. Poor Mandy, mused Amy, trying to hurt herself one devious way after another. Amy had tried. Once. Her attempt had been so serious and so deadly that she knew it would be a long time before she could ever summon up that much courage—or was it mere hopelessness?—again. Slowly, day by day, she was regaining her will to live.

She sat now on the balcony outside the large recreation room. The sun was bright and warm and relaxing, giving Amy a feeling of lethargy. They usually played the television constantly inside, one dreary, depressing soap after another. The game shows were equally inane.

Amy was grateful to be here. Surely she had earned this rest. Sunshine, daily exercise, good food. But, most important, peace and quiet. Here, hidden within the cloistered security of Mount Hope Hospital, she did not have to grapple with those terrifying things that were awaiting her outside these walls. As far as Amy was concerned, she did not want to leave here. She did not want to have to deal with the reality she had left behind.

Amy had been comatose for a week after her stomach was pumped. She lay hovering between life and death with nobody able to predict whether or not she would pull through. They had done all they could, they said, but time would tell if they had reached her in time. Jennifer had found her mother, and that was Amy's biggest regret—next to the fact that she had been found at all and revived. Amy shuddered now, remembering that moment when she first regained consciousness. Oh what an absolutely helpless feeling, strapped to a bed! Her reaction had been, "Let me out of here, turn me loose!" The utter futility created strong and vicious anger, a desire to lash out, kill, destroy. "I'll kill you, I'll kill you!"

Days slipped past as Amy relaxed and had her every need tended by a kind, attentive staff. Her only responsibilities were to get up in the morning and eat her meals at the proper time. Although there was an official bedtime, she was not required to be in bed if she was not sleepy. If she was nervous . . . or upset . . . or depressed . . . or worried . . .all she had to do was approach a staff member. She would then have their undivided attention. Amy liked it here. She never wanted to go home again and have to deal with the insanity that awaited her. At last, she was happy and content.

Or was she? There was another part of Amy that yearned to be free again, yearned to be the productive, contributing person she once was. There was a part that would stand and gaze longingly at the elevator door that would not open without a key, and Amy did not have a key. There was a part of her that rebelled and wanted to scream as she stood in line for medications, little pills to keep her calm so she wouldn't cause any problems. It was always such a sham, knowing she would turn away and spit them out as soon as she was out of sight. Amy had swallowed enough pills to last a lifetime. She would not—indeed, she could not—physically swallow another pill. They would lodge in her throat, its muscles constricting and bringing on a fresh wave of the awful nausea.

"Amy?"

She looked up in the direction of the deep, clear voice, shielding her eyes from the sun. Her heart skipped a beat. "Dr. Wilson!"

The older man slipped into a chair at the little patio table beside her, taking one of her hands into his own. "Amy, dear, how are you?"

Her heart still beat irregularly, wondering about this intrusion into her world, this invasion by that awful reality she had left behind. "Mama?" she whispered. "Is something wrong with Mama?"

"Your mother is fine. We'll talk about her in a moment. But first, tell me about you, Amy. How are you?"

She brought him up to date on her news, skipping the part about how content she was. "I'm coming along just fine."

"And therapy? Are you receiving therapy in here?"

"You mean talking about my problems? Yes, I get to talk about them all I want to. Only . . ."

"Only, what?"

Amy frowned, remembering that empty aching inside. "There's something missing somewhere. I talk all the time but just don't seem to get anywhere. It seems there's a missing key. I don't know."

The two sat in silence for a long moment. Finally the doctor turned to face Amy squarely. "Amy, I want to talk with you now about Dixie."

"I knew something was wrong."

"Dixie's actually doing better, Amy. She's alert, able to track you around the room, and her intelligence is intact. She's sensitive to pain now, and I've been able to communicate with her by letting her blink her eyes. Once for yes, twice for no."

"Oh, doctor, that's wonderful."

"Yes, it is."

"But it means she's still paralyzed."

"I'm afraid so, yes. She is totally immobile except for her ability to move her head in a one-inch radius from a lateral rested position. And her eyes, of course."

"You said you've been able to communicate with her. Has she said anything in particular?"

"As a matter of fact, she indicated that she wanted food and water."

Amy blinked. "Food and water? Isn't she getting those?"

The old doctor nodded. "Of course. And she always will, so long as I'm her attending physician."

Amy sat up straight, gazing directly at the doctor. "Something is wrong; please tell me."

"Amy, I don't know how to say this . . ."

"Just say it. I can take it."

"Can you, Amy?"

"Of course I can! Why shouldn't I?"

Dr. Wilson made a show of looking around, as if to remind Amy of where she was and why. "You made a serious suicide attempt. You've been living in this sheltered environment, away from the outside world. According to your psychiatrist here, you haven't made any efforts to get well so that you can be discharged."

"You talked with Dr. Johnson?"

The doctor looked at Amy for a long time. He sighed. "Obviously you don't know. Dr. Johnson was in court this week. He told the judge what I just told you."

"But why?"

Dr. Wilson studied his fingernails. "Amy, Cliff has petitioned the court to become Dixie's conservator. He seems to feel she has been suffering too much and should be—should be, how can I say?—put out of her misery. When he came to me with this, I refused, so he took me to court. The court, hearing the testimony, has ordered me to have your mother's feeding terminated."

"No!"

"I'm afraid it's true."

"But how can they do that? You just said mother's doing better. How can they do it? Why would Cliff want to do it? I don't understand this. I don't understand any of this!"

"Amy, listen; you need to help us fight."

"How? What can I do?"

"You can start by getting well, so you can get out of this place."

"I am getting well."

Perhaps. But I think you're hibernating in here. I think you're actually putting off getting well, so that you can stay."

A small smile played around Amy's lips. "But I can't—"

"Amy, this is serious. Dixie's done for if we don't fight. We need you."

"What you are saying is incredible. Things like that can't happen."

"Amy, believe me. They can happen and they do."

"It sounds like science fiction."

"The abortion thing, Amy, opened up a whole new way of looking at death. Our world has been conditioned to put a tag of pity on everything that's not convenient."

"What does abortion have to do with my mother?"

The old doctor shook his head. "You too, Amy, have fallen for it. Look at it a moment: is killing an innocent unborn baby really a right? Does it really make you equal to a man? Or does it actually push women's rights backwards? A large majority of men, Amy, advocate abortion because what it really does is exploit women. Men can play all they want to, with no responsibility for the consequences. And yet you women think men have finally accepted you as equals, when all the while they're laughing behind your backs."

"Aren't you exaggerating a bit, doctor?"

"Am I? Abortion is like suicide. It's a cry for help. Many women have abortions, not because of so-called choice, but because of *lack* of choice. Women face so many other crucial issues, and abortion takes the attention off the really important things. You tell me one single pro-abortion agency, Amy, that helps women who decide *not* to abort. They don't. All of that is left for the prolife folks, and because the job is so mammoth, we are criticized because we are not able to accomplish it all."

Amy's shoulders slumped. She herself had done some of that criticizing. She remembered how angry she used to get at prolifers for talking girls out of having abortions without offering anything better. Somehow, she had lost sight of all they *had* offered.

Amy sighed. All her work for abortion rights was down the drain. She had actually been working *against* women's rights. But it all fit. It made perfect, logical sense. "What you're saying, then, Dr. Wilson, is that it's like running down a hill. Once you start, it's awfully hard to put on the brakes."

"Exactly. A slippery slope, Amy. People learn, over time, through conditioning, to accept just about anything that's fed to them. Do you really think people can accept killing unborn babies without eventually expanding it to include others who are just as helpless and in the way— the old, the handicapped? Their quality of life is too poor; they'd be better off dead. Why waste expensive treatment on them?"

"It's just so hard to believe!"

"Look at Dixie. Cliff convinced the court that her living will meant she did not want food and water in this situation."

"But a living will sounded like a good idea to me."

Dr. Wilson nodded. "But it needs to be worded carefully, and it needs to cover all contingencies. We all know what Dixie's wishes were. We know what she meant by heroic measures. But you see, the court interpreted it differently. The judge decided that providing food and water in her case was an unnecessary, heroic measure."

"Someone should put that judge on an extended fast. Wonder how he would like it?"

"Everyone is so involved in so-called rights these days. Someone is always suing someone else over rights. It's like a hot potato, and more and more courts are ruling in favor of these so-called rights. Cliff and his lawyers very eloquently convinced the court that Dixie's right to die is being violated. If this trend continues, the law may eventually allow lethal injections as part of the 'right to die.' "

Amy sat there slumped for a few moments, trying to digest all she had just learned. Her head was spinning with the incredulity of it all. "So you see, Amy, I need you to help us fight."

Amy felt the anger course up her spine, hot and burning. "Why should I be the one always fighting, doctor? Why does Cliff get to chuck all his responsibilities, and then, just as I get to a place where I can start to put my life back together, I've got to start fighting again—all because of him? Why? Why?"

"I don't have an answer, Amy."

"It's not fair!"

"Life is not always fair, Amy. Life is often hard and cruel."

"It's not fair; it's not right. You just wait till I see Cliff Harper. I'll tear him apart at the seams. And that judge, too!"

Dr. Wilson smiled.

17

Amy Fights Again

Miriam bustled around the kitchen, happily humming as she prepared lunch. It was so good to have Ms. Harper back home! It had been a long time since there had really been anyone to cook for.

Amy was in the family room, her feet propped on the coffee table, her lap overflowing with papers. She was going through all the mail that had been accumulating during her stay at Mount Hope.

Bethany remained in her room. Amy had been home all morning, and the girl refused to come out. Finally, when lunch was ready, Miriam padded down the hall to her room and coaxed her to come to the table. She sat facing her mother, silent, not meeting her eyes. They ate quietly for a few moments. "Bethany, how are you feeling these days?"

"Fine."

"Have you been seeing your doctor regularly? You should be going now, what—every other week?"

"I haven't been back to the doctor."

Amy stared at her daughter over a buttered roll. "Why not?"

Bethany shrugged. "I feel fine. I don't need to go."

"Your baby is due in a month, and you aren't seeing a doctor?"

"Mom, leave me alone, will you?"

Amy frowned.

"May I be excused?"

"Beth, I am concerned about your baby, I—"

"You know I don't want it in the first place. You and Daddy wouldn't let me terminate this awful pregnancy. You are forcing me, against my will, to have this baby. But believe you me, as soon as it's born, I'm giving it away."

"Giving it away?"

"I'm giving it away for adoption. I've already picked out the couple."

Suddenly Amy felt so alone. She should have been a part of all these plans for her grandchild. She should have had some input. But now, it seemed everything had been decided without her. Amy could kick herself for that crazy suicide attempt. She really blew it. She had lost out on so much!

"Who's the couple?"

"My English teacher, Mrs. Raymond. They've never been able to have kids, and they're neat people." Bethany made a face. "At least it's getting rid of this—this—" she looked down at her middle, which had grown quite large— "this *thing*."

Amy winced. Is this what she had taught her daughters? "You really don't like your baby, do you?"

"No, and you can't make me. You might force me to have this baby, but you sure can't force me to love it!"

"Listen, young lady; if you'll remember, it was your father who refused to let you have the abortion. It wasn't me."

Bethany stared at her mother. "Well, would you have let me have one?"

"You know what, Beth? Out of my concern for you, I probably would have. I was inclined in that direction. But let's just be glad your father made the decision."

Bethany stared at her mother, her mouth ajar. "Glad!"

"I've learned a lot since then, Bethany. Now I must agree with your father; abortion was not the answer."

"Oh, just leave me alone."

"Bethany, please—"

"May I be excused now?"

Disappointed, Amy excused her daughter. Miriam began to clear the table.

Within a few minutes, Bethany came out of her room, heading for the back door. "I'm going for a ride."

"Ride? Where?"

"I'm going to ride Sultan."

"Ride Sultan?" Sultan was the brain-damaged stallion Cliff kept around. The horse had gotten excited one night and ran off, crashing right into a highway patrol car. He had sustained brain damage, and no one had been able to ride him since. For sentimental reasons, Cliff would not get rid of him.

Amy stared at her daughter, swollen with child, going

to ride a horse. Worse still, going to ride Sultan. She laughed, "Bethany, are you nuts?"

The girl stared at her mother, her eyes glistening with defiance. "I'm quite sane, thank you. You're the one who's been in the nuthouse."

Amy glared at her daughter. "Go to your room."

"I want to ride Sultan."

"I said, go to your room."

"You can't do this."

"Bethany, I'm trying very hard to keep from slapping your silly face."

With that, Bethany turned and stormed down the hall to her room.

* * * * *

Amy was still shaking with fury when she arrived at the nursing home where Granny Dix had been transferred. Rest Haven. Remembering that this was the place where Cliff had originally made arrangements for her mother to stay, Amy steamed inside; Cliff had finally gotten his way, after all. Again, she felt that awful stab of aloneness, of regret, for having bailed out on her family. Again, she had been excluded from the decision making. She felt so left out.

Amy's stomach churned at the odors that taunted her nostrils as she walked down the corridor to her mother's room. There lay Granny Dix, the gray November day casting a depressing shadow across the little room. The woman's face was turned toward the sliding glass doors, and when Amy entered the room, Granny Dix turned her head, very slightly. Her eyes flashed a joyous recognition upon seeing her daughter. Amy hesitated a moment and then ran to her mother's bedside. Grabbing the wrinkled old hand, Amy felt tears coursing down her cheeks, and she made no effort to hide them. "Oh, Mama," she cried, "how are you?"

The old lady just lay there unmoving. Only her eyes spoke, and they spoke kind things like love and joy and glad-to-see-you. The old, gray eyes were the same, deep and clear and knowing. "Mother," she said, "I've missed you so much. Can you understand me?"

Granny Dix was able to nod her head. "But you can't talk yet, can you, Mother?" The head moved, just barely, from side to side. The dear old hand squeezed Amy's tightly. Amy ventured, "Do you know about the court's orders?"

Granny Dix nodded again, a sadness clouding her eyes.

"We did right, didn't we, Mother, giving you this tube? It's your food." Granny Dix nodded, with more vigor this time. "You don't want us to take it away so you can die?"

The large, single tear that fell from her mother's eye said more than a thousand words. The older lady shook her head. To be absolutely certain there was no mistake, Amy pressed on: "Do you want us to help you die, Mother?" An emphatic shaking of the head. "Do you want to live?" And Granny Dix began to nod her head slowly. There was no question.

"Mother, I don't care what that judge says. We will not take this away from you. Do you understand?" Amy looked at her mother, and her heart broke. The dear old cheeks, sunken somewhat and pale, almost gray, were wet with tears of gratitude.

How dare they, raged Amy, order this dear old soul killed!

18

New Deal

The following week it happened. Amy was sitting at her mother's bedside, feeding her tiny drops of food on the tip of a spoon. Amy and Dixie were both ecstatic about the rapid progress in the older woman. She was able to swallow again and was propped up in the bed on a mound of pillows. Her hair had been freshly combed, and she was wearing the red kimono Amy had brought for her eightieth birthday. She still was unable to speak, but her face was alive and regaining its color. She was also able to move her hands and took great advantage of the new freedom by waving them all around in grand communication. "Mother," Amy reproved mockingly, "you must be still! How do you expect me to feed you with you wiggling all around?"

The two women laughed, Dixie's eyes looking like fireworks on the Fourth of July. What a thrill, thought Amy, to see her mother looking so alive again!

The nurse bustled through the door. "Mrs. Harper,

145

there's a phone call for you at the desk."

It was the hospital. Bethany. There had been some kind of accident. Could she come right away?

* * * * *

Bethany had done it after all. Tried to ride that awful stallion. Sultan did not appreciate the intrusion and proceeded to throw the girl across the pasture like a broken rag doll. Now Bethany was in emergency, maybe losing the baby she didn't want in the first place. All Amy could do was wait, here in that same lounge where she had spent all those hours waiting about Granny Dix.

Suddenly, Cliff came in. He looked tired, and old. Fifty? He looked more like sixty-five. Amy felt a stab of satisfaction but then mentally kicked herself. "I just left the doctor," he said. "All we can do is wait." Amy nodded. "While we're waiting," he said, "I need to talk with you."

"About what?"

"Business." Amy glared at him, still filled with resentment that she did not know how to handle.

Amy was surprised at her husband's visible agitation, far removed from the relaxed demeanor he used to have. "Things haven't been doing well, Amy," he said. "It looks like I've got a couple of lawsuits trailing me."

Amy pursed her lips. What did he expect her to say? "We might lose Mothers' Ark," he said abruptly.

Amy blinked. "I'd hate to see that."

"I hate to admit it, but you were right about Lorene. She just split, leaving me holding the bag. I really misjudged her."

"What do you mean?"

"I mean that she's bailed out with all the financial backing—plus leaving a lawyer to carry out her litigation against me."

"What on earth did you do to her?"

Cliff shot her a disgusted look. "Why does everybody assume I did anything to her? She's suing me for fraud. I never lied to her."

"Are you sure?"

He looked at Amy for a moment and then rushed on as though she had never asked a question. "Of course I have all rights to the ranch; she was only its director. But then it will be tied up in the courts, with all these suits pending. I got a tip today, Amy. They're going after everything I own. I've already put the family home in your name so that it will be safe."

"And Mothers' Ark?"

"If you don't mind, I'd like to deed it over to Jennifer right away. Jennifer and Bill and, indirectly, through them, to you and Bethany. In fact, I have all the paperwork right here." Cliff began unloading his briefcase. Amy was startled by this turn of events. Why should they help him out, bail him out of his troubles?

"I know what you're thinking," he said, "but this is to your advantage, too, Amy. You'll all end up owning a substantial property. I've got it all worked out."

"I thought this was a corporation. How are you getting around that?"

"The board has approved everything. It's on the up and up."

Amy felt like kicking herself for helping get him off

the hook; at the same time, her adrenalin began to flow in a way it had not in a long time. There were so many possibilities with the Ark. It was a worthwhile project. Amy thought of her own little Bethany, pregnant and unmarried. That was the kind of girl who lived at the Ark. Where would these girls go if the Ark closed down? What would happen to them? Suddenly her heart did a flip, and she felt like rolling up her sleeves and digging in to build something.

But there was the case of Granny Dix. "What about Mother?" she asked.

Cliff squirmed against the leather seat. "What about her?"

"Are you going to pursue killing her?"

"Amy! It's not killing her, for heaven's sake."

Amy did not wish to argue the point. "Well, are you going to pursue it or drop it?"

"There's nothing to pursue. The court has ordered that they stop torturing her and let her die in peace."

"Cliff Larue Harper! You are totally deceived! You are a rat!"

"I can understand," he said calmly, "how you would feel that way."

Amy shook her head in disbelief. What had happened to the man she married thirty years ago? Where did he go?

"I have here," he said, reaching into his coat pocket, "a check for fifty thousand dollars. You need to deposit it; then have Jen write a check out to Mothers' Ark in the same amount."

Amy stared at the check. "Whose money is this?"

"It's from the board."

"It says Camden Company."

"Right. They're paying Jen for a piece of property they are purchasing from her."

Amy felt blown away. "What property? She doesn't have any property."

Cliff smiled. "Honey, she's owned a piece of land in the mountains for the past ten years. Only on paper, of course. It was something I worked out in one of my deals."

Amy sighed. She had never been able to keep abreast of Cliff and his deals. They had always been complicated, detailed affairs, over her head. She took the check, folded it up, and placed it in her purse. "You're sure all this is legal?"

"I want you and the girls to have it. It's important to me. It would end up being lost, anyhow, so please. Just accept it."

"What are the lawsuits for?"

"Don't worry about them. They're my problem; I'll take care of them."

"Cliff, what happened? You had everything going for you."

He gave her a long serious look, and for just a moment, Amy thought this was the old Cliff she used to know. "The beginning of the end," he said solemnly, "was when I looked at another woman. Hearts are something we can't afford to play around with. I never dreamed I'd lose mine. I thought I was tough, impervious. But I lost my heart—along with you and everything else. I blew it, Amy. That's all."

Amy was thrilled that he was talking to her from his innermost being, but just as suddenly as he had started talking, he moved on to other subjects. Amy allowed him to ramble for a few moments and then brought the conversation back to the concern of her own heart. "About my mother. Are you going to drop it, or not?"

"Amy, it's gone far beyond me. I don't even have to lift a finger. There are organizations—big ones—that believe, as I do, that Dr. Wilson and that nursing home—and you, too, if you get involved—are depriving Dixie of her rights."

"And so these organizations, who don't even know my mom, plan on fighting for her rights."

"They want to make a new law, Amy. People's basic rights are at stake."

"Mama's right to be killed . . ."

"Amy, again—it's not killing . . ."

"Cliff, I want to ask you something."

"Sure."

"Do you really believe what you're saying?"

Cliff just stared at her. He had no answer to her question.

"Say, hey!" Both heads turned to see a smiling nurse. "It's all over. Mother and baby are both doing fine." Amy's hand found itself nestled in Cliff's. It was all over. In just a few short moments, they had become grandparents.

19

Away with the Old

Dr. Wilson was on the phone. "They were here again today, Amy, trying to get me to disconnect Dixie's food."

"But why? I talked to Cliff, and he said he was out of it."

"Some organization called Death with Dignity is suing me personally for not killing your mother. They told me to pack my toothbrush and be ready to go to jail if I did not comply."

"Jail?" What a ludicrous picture Amy thought: this kind and distinquished physician in jail!

"Amy, I don't want to go to jail."

"Well, I don't blame you; I wouldn't either. But what about mother? You're not going to comply, are you?" Amy held her breath. "I mean—"

"Of course not."

Amy had never felt such helplessness in her life. She thought surely she must be in the middle of a nightmare and would wake up any minute now.

The sound of a car in the driveway shattered her reverie. It was Cliff bringing Bethany home. Bethany and her new baby. The agreement had been that the adopting parents take the baby home with them, but for some reason, they were unavailable. Amy sighed, squared her shoulders, and prepared for the ordeal ahead.

After Bethany was settled in her room, Amy bustled around with the baby. Little Cecily, she was called. Amy warmed a bottle and cuddled on the couch, she and the baby. The tiny little lips pursed around the nipple of the bottle, and Amy's heart skipped a beat. This little tyke looked just like Bethany did as a newborn! Amy sat there staring at the baby, the tiny little girl that had such a struggle coming into this world. But she was a fighter, this one, and had broken down all barricades standing in the way of her grand entrance.

As Amy sat studying the tiny features, she realized with a start that mothers had abortions with babies this size. She knew that; she had helped fight for that right. Now she sat in abject terror. "My God, my God," she whispered, "what have I done?" Instinctively she held her little granddaughter tighter. Wave after wave of revelation swept over her. "Abortion is killing," she whispered into the hushed room. "It really is killing. . . ."

And in that moment she knew. Amy became vividly aware of the specter of death that had stalked her since she had herself killed her little son those thirty years ago. Although she had repressed it and refused to deal with it, still the experience had remained lodged within her, the experience of having killed her own flesh and blood. No matter her motivation; no matter her lack of knowledge. Because Amy surely had not thought of her baby as a baby—not a real baby—when she had that abortion so long ago. She had not really thought of it as anything at all, except a real problem. And when she heard that there was a minor surgical procedure that could eliminate the problem with minimal risk to her, Amy had agreed.

It was done in a safe and sterile office by a licensed medical doctor. Part of the feminists' rhetoric these days, she knew, was that illegal abortions had all been done in a back alley, on a butcher's kitchen table somewhere. She knew about that rhetoric, because she had printed a lot of it in *She* magazine. But just because something was printed, she realized in a flash, did not make it true and accurate.

Even though she and Cliff had eloped when she learned she was pregnant, Cliff was just starting out in business and simply could not afford to start a family just then. Amy, disheartened and discouraged, understood. She also wanted the security that a well-paid husband could provide. There would be time later, they reasoned together, for having a family. Later, after they had acquired a home and a reasonable income, a baby would have a far better chance of success and happiness. Right now, though, it would be so hard, they concluded, not only on Cliff and Amy, but also on a newborn baby. They decided the baby was better off dead than second-class, Amy now thought bitterly.

And so the decision was made. The little baby was put to rest.

But the bond was already there, that fragile yet eternal bond between a mother and her offspring. That bond was cut off and denied the chance to grow and mature. But it was not destroyed. It would always be there, because the baby was a living soul. The bond was between two living souls, not between a woman and her own body. Suddenly Amy had another frightening revelation: the baby was not a part of his mother's body. That notion was incredible. Her own experience had proved that. If that baby had been a part of Amy's body, why was it so complete and self-contained at its termination?

Amy was gripping her tiny granddaughter in her arms as she went back in time to that afternoon in the motel where she had gone to recuperate after her abortion.

* * * * *

The heavy curtains were drawn, and the hum of the air conditioner seemed deafening. She was alone; Cliff was still at work.

Amy had turned her head into the big pillow and felt a tear slide down her cheek onto the crisp, white pillowcase. She couldn't understand these feelings. Why was she so empty inside? So lonely? She had only had a minor surgical procedure, but she was having a lot of pain, with cramping sensations. She hurriedly got up to take some of the pills Jeff, the doctor, had given her for pain.

When she went to the bathroom, she had a strange sensation and looked down into the toilet bowl. She wished she never had, for what she saw there would haunt her for the rest of her life. It looked like a large blood clot. She scooped it up and stared at it, mesmerized. This must be the tissue she had heard about. But the closer she looked at it, the less it looked like plain tissue. It was more like—. She spun around to the lavatory and rinsed it off under running water. Then the horror of what she had done slapped her in the face. Because what she held in her hand was not mere tissue. It was not a blood clot. What she held in her hand was a real human being!

Her head spinning, she stumbled back to the bed, continuing to cling to the tiny dead being in the palm of her hand. Fighting down her fears, her eyes searched the tiny creature. Perfect fingers and toes. Perfect in every way. And a little boy! This was her son. Heaven help her, what had she done!

After she sat there, awestruck, for what seemed like hours, she heard Cliff's key in the lock. As he entered the room, she could not look at him. He knew instinctively that something was wrong and came and sat down beside her on the large bed. "Honey? Are you okay?" She nodded, her eyes not meeting his. "Amy?" She still could not meet his eyes, and his hand reached up, turning her chin towards him. "Honey, are you okay? Talk to me."

She threw herself into his arms and wept. "Please," she wept, "please just hold me and let me cry."

"But what's wrong?"

She opened her hand and displayed their little son for him to see. She wasn't prepared for his reaction. His blue eyes narrowed and his jaw tightened, stiff as steel. "Go flush that thing down the john."

"No!"

He sighed and tried to reason with her in that patient, condescending tone he used so well. "It's doing you no good to torture yourself like this. We've got to put this behind us."

She stared at him numbly. And she knew it would not do any good to talk further. She knew that he was convinced that the worst possible thing that could happen to her would be to talk about this experience. He felt that it would hurt her too much to discuss the little son she held in her hands. He felt it would only cause her grief and pain, and he didn't want that. He wanted her to put it all behind her so she wouldn't have to experience these ugly emotions. He meant well.

She squared her shoulders and closed her heart. Numbly, she asked, "Will you at least have a funeral for him?"

"Amy!"

"Well? Will you?"

"Honey, you're being morbid. Of course we'll have no funeral. Don't be silly."

"Look at him," she whispered, holding the tiny baby toward her husband. He jerked his head away. "Look at him, Cliff; look at your son!"

Cliff stood up abruptly and began removing his jacket and tie. His movements were jerky, distracted. Wordlessly, Amy pulled her robe tightly around her and went out onto the little patio. The sun was still hot and bright, and she fought the dizziness that was swirling through her head. And there in the little garden, among the roses and a couple of azaleas, she dug a hole and placed her little son inside. She would not let herself whisper to him, nor would she let herself feel. She mechanically went through the motions and then went back into the motel room. "Let's go home," she said.

And so they went home, leaving all her feelings buried

with her tiny little son among the roses. Determined to put it out of her mind forever. . . .

* * * * *

But had she? Just because she didn't think about it did not mean it was out of her mind. She had read a pro-life pamphlet once that had sent her up the wall in fury. It said that many times women who have abortions become prochoice, not because they believe abortion is a good thing, but because they, having killed their own babies and thus having been deprived of them, could not bear to see another woman rise victoriously above her circumstances by facing the problem, working out solutions, and giving birth to her baby. Sickened, Amy realized this to be true.

Amy reflected on the old Bible story of King Solomon and the two women who claimed to be mother of the same baby. "Cut him in two," said the wise old king, "and divide him equally between the two women." One woman agreed with this solution; the other woman begged not to have the child slain and was willing to relinquish him to the other woman. Only spare him, don't kill him. And King Solomon knew who the real mother was.

In a flash, Amy recognized the modern-day implications. And in a flash she realized just how deeply it hurt to witness other women showing strength where she had shown only weakness. This was a psychological issue that went beyond the training of the standard psychotherapist. It was complex, because it belonged to the arena of death. She saw with a start just how closely abortion was related to the nightmare with Granny Dix. Dr. Wilson knew exactly what he was talking about!

Amy's face flamed with shame at her abject cowardice, her petty selfishness, and she wanted to crawl into a hole so that no one would ever find out. Surely she could never face anyone, not ever again! She had been working for the so-called good of women when she herself was so utterly selfish and self-centered! What gall, what nerve!

But strangely, even as she felt that the shame would engulf and annihilate her, there seemed to be something even stronger washing over her. As she faced herself at last and came face to face with the truth, tears began to bring a form of healing to her soul. She felt lighter and cleaner with each tear, and she made no effort to stop them. Somehow, in some way, she knew that, at last, she would be all right.

20

Cecily Finds a Home

Amy heard a sound at the door. There stood Bethany, still looking fresh-faced after all she had gone through. She was standing there now staring at Amy. "Mom, you're crying."

Amy smiled through her tears. "Maybe a little."

"Because of Cecily?"

"In a way, I suppose you could say that." Amy smiled again, patting the couch beside her. Bethany slipped across the room and sat beside her mother. "Want to hold her?"

"You think it would be all right?"

"You haven't held her yet? In the hospital?"

"No. I was expecting the Raymonds to come and take her home, and I didn't want to see her."

"You can hold your baby if you want to."

Bethany nodded, taking the infant into her arms. "Mom," she whispered in wonder, "She's so tiny."

"Tiny but sturdy," said Amy. "She's a little fighter."

Bethany smiled down proudly at her child, and Amy asked, "Were they ever able to locate the Raymonds?"

"They are on vacation. Mr. Haynes, the principal, said they took an early vacation so they'd be sure to be around when it was time for my baby to be born. Ironic, huh? Say, Mom?"

"Hm-m?"

"I'm sorry. For all the trouble I've caused. And for trying to ride that stupid horse. I've been a real brat."

"I understand."

"I'm serious, Mom. I've been a *Brat,* with a capital B."

"Well, it's all behind us now."

The infant let out a little cry, and Bethany rushed to put the bottle in her mouth. As she fed her baby, she sat in silence, running her finger around the tiny eyes and mouth and nose. Amy quietly witnessed the scene and was not surprised to hear the next words. "Mom, I've been thinking. And I am glad you and Daddy didn't let me have that abortion."

"How is that?"

"Things have changed, Mom. I look at this little girl and see how helpless she is. She wouldn't have stood a chance against an abortion."

"That's right."

"I'm so glad! Look, Mom, she's alive. I gave her life!"

Amy cringed, knowing that Bethany would probably not be able to say that had it been left up to Amy. "Yes, you gave her life, Bethany, and for that you can be free for the rest of your life. You won't have to live with the specter of death stalking you. You can live with peace, not with sorrow."

"According to what the clinic at school told us, Mom, my baby shouldn't be getting all this love."

"How come?"

"They say that a girl shouldn't be forced to have an unwanted baby, because the baby will become an unloved, abused baby. And goodness knows, I sure didn't want my baby."

"I'm starting to believe, Bethany, that there's no such thing as an unwanted baby."

"Jen was right about the school clinic. She tried to warn me not to believe all their garbage."

Amy looked at her daughter for a long moment. "Tell me about this clinic. What do they do there besides dispense contraceptives and perform abortions?"

"They don't actually do abortions there on the school grounds—at least not yet. I've heard that a lot of the clinics do, and this one's applying for the money to do it here. They refer," explained Bethany. "And they arrange for the kids to get time off from school. They drive the kids to their appointments. I get the feeling that they really don't want the parents to know."

"Do you know why?"

"Some kids have parents who hit the ceiling. Some have parents like you and Dad who won't let them go through with it. I know one thing."

"What's that?"

"They sure cause a lot of confusion. Especially my Family Life class. Sometimes my head would swim because I'd get so mixed up. Especially about you and Daddy. They'd teach us things that made it hard to trust you guys sometimes."

"Can you give me an example?"

Bethany studied her fingernails, which were growing long again. "You and Daddy said it's a bad idea to have sex before marriage."

"What do they say?"

"That it's a good idea, because it does away with fear and guilt."

Amy could barely speak, but she wanted to hear more about this. She swallowed. "What else?"

"Well, you always told me to control myself. They say we need to let go and do whatever feels good. They say control causes inhibitions and messes up our minds."

"Maybe you just misunderstood, Beth. I'm sure they must have meant it differently."

"No they did not, either. All the kids heard it the same way. And later when we asked about it, they said it again."

Amy was shocked. No wonder the girl had grown hard and rebellious. No wonder she had ended up pregnant. Amy again felt that awful shame creep over her, this time the shame of sheer blindness. She had been so deceived! She could see so clearly now that she had missed her life's calling; she had missed the will of God. No wonder she was so miserable and empty inside; she had spent a lifetime running from herself!

Instead of fulfilling her call as a wife and mother, she had been off chasing rainbows and changing laws. Instead of tending the fires of home and school, she had battled windmills that existed only in the chambers of her mind. And instead of fighting for the right to decency and morality for those who meant the most to her, she had been off crusading for rights that weren't even rights at all. Oh, the sheer nonsense of it all!

* * * * *

If little Cecily had ever been unwanted by her birth mother, her adopting parents made up all the slack. Amy was overjoyed to meet the Raymonds and witness their genuine, unbounded love for little Cecily. This was Amy's first grandchild, and she would always hold a special place in her heart. No other child could ever fill that place. Now she could understand how her own mother felt about Jennifer.

The adoption process was hard on everybody. Bethany had grown to love her little daughter and found it difficult to let her go. But she kept reminding herself that she was doing the best thing for Cecily. Bethany had talked it over with friends and family. She had undergone counseling at the open adoption center. She had agonized over the decision. And in the end, she felt, down deep in her heart, that giving Cecily up would be the most loving, unselfish way of resolving the dilemma.

The teenager stood by the front window, her nose pressed against the glass, watching as little Cecily rode away with her new parents. Once, twice, she started to change her mind. Finally, she turned from the window and looked squarely at Amy. "Well, she's gone, Mom. But I gave her life."

Amy watched her daughter. Bethany had grown a lot from this, matured, and developed spiritually. Her granddaughter had gone on to another life, but her daughter had reentered hers. The sadness Amy felt was acute and very real, but just under the surface of it all was a deep, abiding joy.

As soon as she could, Amy went out to visit Granny Dix. She needed her mother now and sank beside her bed. Dixie understood without words and moved her arms so that Amy could rest her head on her breast. For a long time Amy remained that way, unmoving, just gaining strength from her mother.

After awhile, without moving, Amy spoke. "Oh, Mama, I've made such a mess of my life. I've been an awful mother; you just wouldn't believe. No wonder Cliff walked out on me." Amy felt her mother's hand stroking her hair, and suddenly lonesomeness for her little dead son overwhelmed her. "Mother, a long time ago I did something I regret more than anything in the world. It's tearing me up, Mama."

Amy heard a rasping sound. Her heart stopped beating for just a minute. What was that? She listened intently. It was her mother, talking! "No need to be tormented," came the tired old voice. "Give it to the Lord."

Amy sat up straight. "Mama! You're talking!" Granny Dix's face lit up with a glow Amy had thought she would never see again. "Does it hurt you to talk?"

Granny Dix shook her head and pressed on persistently. Her words became stronger with each breath. "He will forgive you, Amy May. Give it to Him. And then get on with living."

Amy felt like crying. "You don't understand, Mama. What I did was really, really bad. One of the worst sins there is."

"I don't care how bad it was. He wants to forgive you. You need the Lord, Amy May. Your way hasn't worked."

"Oh, Mama . . . He can't forgive me for this."

"Once you were filled with the Holy Spirit, Amy, and took His name on you in baptism. You are His child. Give it to Him."

"Dixie!" The sound from the door startled both women, and they looked up to see Dr. Wilson. "Praise God!" he bellowed. "You're doing it, Dixie. You're talking!"

21

New Beginnings

Amy remembered the day that seemed so long ago now, the hot summer afternoon when she had stood in this very spot and watched Cliff and Lorene together. Now she was alone, just her and a chilly winter breeze of a cold but sunny day. The house was just as lovely as it had been last summer. Only this time it belonged to her and her children, and she did not feel like an intruder.

Amy's eyes swept to that wide front veranda, the one where she had once expected to see Scarlett O'Hara appear. There was a figure there now, sitting tall and serene, a deep-rose shawl draped across small and delicate shoulders. The old woman was breathing deeply of the cold, dry air, a look of gratitude for being alive spread across her face. Her countenance seemed to glow, even from a distance. Granny Dix. Alive and well, moving among the living, making daily contributions of love and compassion, ministering as she could among the young and single mothers-to-be of Mothers' Ark.

Amy laughed out loud, the sound of her laughter carrying up to the veranda. Granny Dix raised a hand and waved a greeting to her daughter. Amy started walking toward the veranda, a feeling of lightness and freedom carrying her along. For the first time that she could remember, Amy was truly happy.

The sound of a car attracted her attention. Jennifer and Billy were back from their shopping trip, loaded down with goodies for the home and for the residents. They had decided to move back to Lawton last month. Life in the capital was not what they had envisioned, and Amy was so thankful that Billy had a work to do, right here at Mothers' Ark. He was ecstatic: "Sounds like just the job for me," he said, "taking care of all the animals."

Jennifer had thrown her head back, laughing. "Oh, Mom, you should have seen how out of place my husband looked in Sacramento! Daddy was right about that business suit. It's just not for Billy."

Jennifer had enrolled in the university in Lawton and was busily involved in classes. Her exposure to the political life in Sacramento had only served to whet her appetite, and she was now more excited than ever about her future in politics. Her candidate had won, and she was watching the wheels of justice begin to turn as she had dreamed during all those lonely campaign hours. But Amy was hesitant. Politics could be cruel. She would wait and see.

Amy had never pictured herself in this kind of management either, and she sometimes wondered what on earth she was doing, trying to run this home. She had had very little training in the business world, and her people skills left a lot to be desired. But with everyone supporting her it was all pulling together somehow.

Granny Dix looked at Amy now as Jennifer stepped onto the porch. "I just can't get over it," she said.

"What's that, Mama?"

"Being alive. It's almost sinful, isn't it?—having such a zest for life at my age."

"I think it's beautiful."

"Me, too," agreed Jennifer. "Oh, by the way, Mom, I just heard some news in town about Daddy." Everyone turned to look at Jennifer. "I heard that no one had been able to locate him. There are a bunch of lawyers looking for him; did you know that?" Amy nodded. "Anyway, it looks as if he's just disappeared. Not a trace. Strange, huh, Mom?"

"In a way, yes. But he had a lot of pressure on him, Jen. Be patient with your dad. When he's ready, he'll be back. Be patient."

"Mom," said Jennifer, "I used to have my doubts about you."

"Doubts? How come?"

"I used to think you'd never make it without Daddy. But looks to me like you're doing just fine."

"Of course she is," piped in Granny Dix. "Jenny's learning that her true fulfillment, her real contentment, is all in the Lord."

"Jenny?"

"Who did I say?"

"You said Jenny."

"Well, you know who I meant. Amy May."

Amy laughed. "I only wonder, Mama—why did I wait so long? . . . Where's Billy?"

"Down at the hangar." Amy had caused a small flying strip to be built on a section of the land that looked as though it was made to be a runway. Flat and level, sheltered from the worst of the winds, it was perfect.

"What's he doing down there?"

"Checking your plane over. He says it's time, Mom."

Amy shook her head. "Not yet."

"He says it is. I agree."

Granny Dix decided to jump into the conversation. "And so do I!"

All eyes turned to Granny Dix, opened wide in surprise. "You do?"

"Of course. Can't a woman change her mind?" The family broke out in laughter. "How many seats you got in that little thing?"

"Four," said Amy.

"See? One for you. One for Billy. One for Jenny. And one for . . . me."

"You!"

"Sure enough. Let's fly!"

Amy gazed at her mother, the same little woman who had maintained that she would never, ever set foot inside a private aircraft. Where had this sudden surge of courage come from? Amy was thrilled. But she was so frightened. She had tried to fly several times since her plane was repaired. Each time, as she took her place in the left seat, an unreasonable fear overwhelmed her. Her palms began to sweat, and she started hearing those awful sounds of crashing metal and glass. And she had simply not been able to start the engine.

Amy looked at the faces that were watching her expectantly. Faces that had confidence in her, faces that trusted in her. Faces that believed she could do anything she set her mind to—even fly again. Billy's voice came echoing from the hangar, and Amy turned to follow the sound. Without a word, she thrust out her chin and began marching down to the field strip, her skirt whipping around her knees, followed by her mother and her daughter. Three generations climbed inside the little plane and shut out the world as they shut the doors.

Amy, a radiant smile across her face, started the engine and taxied to the strip. The sound of the rpm thrilled her heart, sending contentment coursing through the very marrow of her bones. She turned the plane into the wind and revved its engine. As the Cessna rolled down the runway, two clear, gray eyes peered out from the back seat, two gray eyes filled with the apprehension of the first plane ride . . . but also with the absolute wonder of beginning a brand-new adventure, embarking on a brand-new life. At age eighty. Goodbye, Granny Dix.

If you have had an abortion or know someone who has, this special section is written just for you. Like Nancy in *Lisa Said No* and like Amy in *Goodbye, Granny Dix,* I too had an abortion. My story is told in chapter 19. That was the way it happened in my life. Like Amy, I too buried my grief along with my little son. Also like Amy, the sorrow and grief would not stay buried. All women who commit this act must one day be confronted with it. Better to do it now, and begin to live a life that God can fully use, than to continue through life crippled.

One woman had several abortions in her past. When she first came into the truth, she received it joyfully and her initial walk with God was a good one. But she was unable to give her abortions to Jesus for healing. She never felt forgiveness, and she remained fragmented in her mind. Today she is backslidden, still fragmented, and her mind filled with delusions that have been hurtful to the body of Christ.

The aftermath of abortion can cause many things to go wrong in a person's life, things that often border on the insane. The reason for this is that abortion, unlike other sins that we can so readily give to Jesus, involves willful destruction of our very own flesh-and-blood offspring. It is the physical severing of a bond that can never be severed emotionally. It involves what psychologists call repression. But like the little leaven, it must be purged. Here is the story of how God purged me. This kind of healing is available to anyone who wants it. It can be yours.

Like Amy, it all began when I held my first grand-child in my arms. My progeny. The whole concept was suddenly awesome. This child was my child, flesh of my flesh, and the sudden realization swept over me that God creates all relationships. His perfect plan for our lives and families fits together like pieces of a puzzle, and when we willfully destroy one of those pieces, nothing fits quite right. Something is wrong. When I looked into the precious, little face of my grandson, I began to realize the enormity of what I had done so many years ago.

The next thing happened during a regular Sunday morning church service. I was seated in the congregation worshiping God when I happened to look up on the platform. As music director, my son Joseph was in his usual place at the organ. Next to him, almost at his elbow, stood another young man I had never seen before. I was perplexed, wondering why he was on the platform. He was tall, handsome, a godly-looking young man in his early twenties. Although I didn't recognize him, he did look strangely familiar.

Then his eyes met mine, and the Holy Ghost spoke to my heart. I knew that this vision represented the little son I had aborted those long years ago! His eyes did not hold hatred for me, only concern; and just as suddenly as he had appeared, he disappeared. Floodgates opened, and I began to weep. God was there, holding me, and I wept through the remainder of the service. Weeping is not unusual in a Pentecostal service, so no one disturbed me. My brothers and sisters just allowed me the luxury of tears, and I know many of them were praying for me as I wept. I wept for days. I realized I was going through something, but I didn't know what, because at that time I didn't know the first thing about counseling women who had had abortions.

I wrote a letter to my pastor, confessing my abortion. I wrote because writing is easier for me but also because I didn't want to put him in a position of having to respond, of feeling he had to do something. I just wanted him to be aware that I was going through some sort of grieving process. My pastor is caring and compassionate, and I feel that I can talk to him freely. But abortion is a complex issue; it is not a comfortable thing to deal with women who have this kind of problem. Although I know he could have dealt with it, I saw no reason to put him on the spot. I did ask for prayer. Prayer changes things, and there is nothing more effective than a praying shepherd!

I continued to let God have His way. Tears cleanse and heal, and I allowed them to flow freely during every service. And like Job of old, I worshiped. The key to the whole mystery of healing is worship. While we have our eyes and mind on Jesus, He can do wonders with the inside of us!

And so this is the pathway I found to healing. Tears. Confession that led to repentance. Worship. Putting my self into the loving hand of God. Total submission to Him, and a commitment to letting Him do this work in my life and those secret rooms in my heart.

If you are already part of a Spirit-filled congregation, you are on your way. If not, look for such a church and become a part of it. Join in the services. Sing, clap your hands, worship, praise. Ask God to give you the same healing and wholeness that He gave to me. And then expect it. Accept it when it comes. And thank Him with your whole heart. Because there is a new life ahead for you, beyond your wildest dreams. I know. I have found it.

If after reading GOODBYE, GRANNY DIX, you would like to communicate with the author, you may write to her at

125 West Central Avenue, Box D
Madera, California 93637.

Lynda speaks to various groups on many topics, and would be happy to talk with you about ministering to YOUR group.